TWO-GUN LAW

Center Point
Large Print

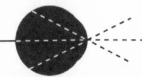

**This Large Print Book carries the
Seal of Approval of N.A.V.H.**

TWO-GUN LAW

Clifton Adams

CENTER POINT LARGE PRINT
THORNDIKE, MAINE

This Center Point Large Print edition
is published in the year 2014 by arrangement with
Golden West Literary Agency.

The text of this Large Print edition is unabridged.
In other aspects, this book may vary
from the original edition.
Printed in the United States of America
on permanent paper.
Set in 16-point Times New Roman type.

ISBN: 978-1-62899-349-3 (hardcover)
ISBN: 978-1-62899-356-1 (paperback)

Library of Congress Cataloging-in-Publication Data

Adams, Clifton.
Two-gun law / Clifton Adams. — Center Point Large Print edition.
pages ; cm
Summary: "Jeff Denfield goes to Texas with his Civil War comrade to
help him regain his ranch and ends up in a battle for his life"—Provided
by publisher.
ISBN 978-1-62899-349-3 (hardcover : alk. paper) — ISBN 978-1-
62899-356-1 (pbk. : alk. paper)
1. Large type books. I. Title.
PS3551.D34T88 2014
813'.54—dc23
                                                        2014028585

Chapter One

The day General Lee put down his sword at Appomattox a great many of us lost the only steady job we'd ever had. Not many of us were sorry. Soldiering for the Confederacy had lost a good deal of its glitter by that time. Empty bellies and threadbare uniforms and one bloody defeat after another had pretty well convinced us that we were fighting on borrowed time.

One day the cannons stopped their bellowing, and the Major rode down from Appomattox Courthouse and told us that the Army of Northern Virginia had surrendered. He was only a kid himself, the Major. A slight, towheaded boy of twenty-two whose father was a senator or governor or something. Great fat tears flowed over the red rims of his eyes and slithered down his pinkish cheeks into the scraggly blond beard that he had cultivated so carefully. The Major took it hard. The rest of us were merely embarrassed.

That same night Phil Carney, gunnery officer of C Battery, came back from the Courthouse with a bottle of Yankee whisky, three lemons, and a pound of coffee; items almost unheard of in the South. To get them, he had given a Yankee sutler a brace of silver-mounted dueling pistols that were worth at least two hundred dollars, hard money.

"Are you crazy?" I said.

"Sure." He grinned. "What would you have done? Let the Yankees steal them?"

"Officers get to keep their side arms, I hear."

"If they're as valuable as those dueling pistols? Not unless human nature has changed, and that I seriously doubt. Here." He threw a lemon at me, the first fruit I had seen in almost a year. I built up the small campfire and filled the bucket and set it on to boil with the coffee.

"Smell that coffee!" Phil Carney said, working at the cork in the whisky bottle. "I haven't smelled anything like that since I left Texas."

There was a go-to-hell attitude about Carney that I had always liked, although it kept both of us in trouble most of the time. His age was twenty-one, which was at least two years older than he looked, and he had a wide mouth that grinned most of the time, even when there was nothing to grin about. He was a long, gawky kid who fought savagely and with great enthusiasm, as though he were anxious to get the war over with and get on to something else. Only by the unpredictable grace of God had he survived three years of fighting.

"Eat the lemon," he said, throwing away the peel of one he had already devoured, and I laughed.

"Don't you ever save anything for tomorrow?"

"Tomorrow the Yankees might change their minds and start fightin' again. Eat the lemon."

I ate it, almost contracting lockjaw as the sour

juices flowed over my tongue. Then, passing me the bottle, Carney insisted that we wash the coffee down with whisky. It was the only way he knew to live. Squeeze every drop out of today and let tomorrow take care of itself.

"What are you going to do," I said after a while, "now that the war is over?" I handed the bottle back to him.

"Go back to God's country." He grinned. "Back to Texas."

"After the fighting, won't that be kind of quiet?"

"It's never quiet in Texas," he said.

I had never liked many men the way I had got to like Phil Carney. It could be said truthfully that we owed our lives to each other, for more than once I had saved him from the consequences of battle-inflamed bravery, and he had done the same for me. Still, it was not because of the kid alone that I had more or less stuck to him and watched after him through three years of fighting.

Phil Carney had a sister. Just how or when she had stepped out of nowhere to take a place in my life, I neither knew nor understood. All I knew about Laura Carney was that she was two years older than her brother, and she had dark hair and a small oval-shaped face, according to a faded daguerreotype picture that the kid carried with him in a locket. She seemed beautiful to me, although the condition of the picture made it impossible to be certain about that. Maybe it was because men at war don't get a chance to see many women. Anyway, without Laura Carney's consent—without even knowing her—I had somehow begun thinking of her as mine.

And now I was telling myself that it was time to get my feet on the ground again. Laura had served her purpose. Men at war need something to think about and keep them in touch with reality. Something to hold them when they start over the deep end of savagery. A home, a wife, a family. I had none of those things, so for those three years I had taken Laura Carney, through her letters to her brother—which the kid always read aloud—through the faded picture in the locket, and in other various and more subtle ways that I did not completely understand.

But now the war was over, and I was learning that a dream can be a hard thing to turn loose. At the age of thirty-four I felt like an old man.

"What do you aim to do, Jeff?" the kid said, handing me the whisky bottle and a tin cup full of rare steaming coffee.

"Do?" I thought for a minute. "The same thing I've always done, I guess. Ride the river from St. Louis to New Orleans, and then back again."

"Gamblin'?"

"It's all I know. I don't expect the river will be the same, though, as it was before the war."

Then, thoughtfully: "Have you ever thought of comin' to Texas?"

I was glad that it was dark, for I could feel the color rising to my face. I realized then that I had been fishing for an invitation ever since the news of the surrender. Drop it, I thought. Laura Carney isn't likely to be the kind of girl to take to a professional gambler. Stick to the forty-niners and fancy girls in the dance halls and saloons. They're more your type, Denfield.

I managed a laugh, but it didn't sound quite right. "What would a man like me do in Texas?"

The kid studied the sinking level of whisky in the bottle. "No law against gamblin' in Texas." Then, glancing sidewise at me, he grinned. "Course, you may have a tougher time of it down there than you would ridin' the Mississippi. Texans have a habit of doin' things big, includin' gamblin'."

He looked at me, then he lay back on his elbows and stared into the fire, saying nothing more about my coming with him. Maybe he hadn't meant it at all, I thought. Maybe he was just kidding. You never knew about Phil Carney. Then he seemed to forget that I was there, and he took out that locket and opened it and studied it thoughtfully, as he sometimes did when he was alone. Although I knew it was ridiculous, a feeling of envy and jealousy swept over me, but I tried to hide it as he snapped the locket shut and said mildly, "I forgot to tell you, Jeff. My sister asked about you in her last letter."

9

I felt uncomfortable and didn't know what to say, and I was glad to hear the heavy tramp of infantry boots coming toward us, hoping that it was someone who could help me change the line of conversation. A big shadow fell across the lighted area and a hoarse voice said:

"By God, I could smell that coffee clean over to A Battery," and I didn't have to look up to know who it was. His name was Johnston—Howard A. Johnston, Captain, C.S.A., better known as Big Belly Johnston to the men of his company. He had a raw-red face, big paddle feet, and a tremendous belly, and was given up to be one of the most talented foragers in the Confederate Army of Northern Virginia. No one liked him or wanted him around, but he always appeared where there was rumor of food or drink, and few men dared turn him away, for Captain Howard A. (Big Belly) Johnston was big and tough and he was a fighter.

He was saying now, with a forced heartiness that made me squirm, "Damme if I didn't guess it! Clean over to A Battery I smells this coffee, and I says to myself, 'Howard, by God, that there's coffee, real honest-to-God coffee, damme if it ain't! Some pore old Johnny Reb's plain got hisself hold of some Yankee coffee!' That's just what I said!"

"All right," Phil Carney said wearily. "Help yourself to what's left in the bucket."

"Just happened to bring my cup with me," Captain Johnston said, dipping happily into the bucket with a blackened tin cup. Luckily he hadn't seen the whisky bottle, so I threw my blanket over it and prepared to put up with Howard until the coffee ran out.

"By God," Johnston said, "you boys know how to live! I never taste coffee like this since I left Georgia. Say," he nodded to Phil Carney, "what's that trinket you've got there?"

The kid had been idly twirling the locket in his fingers, not paying much attention to Johnston. Without warning, Big Belly reached out with a bearlike paw and plucked the locket out of Carney's fingers. Before the kid could speak, the Captain had opened the locket and was peering at the picture with his small, pinkish eyes.

"Well, well!" he said, flashing a yellow-toothed grin. "Now, that's a pert little piece, all right! Who is she, kid? One of your dance-hall sweeties back in Richmond?"

An unreasoning rage went over me. I didn't even see the kid as he came suddenly to his knees, fists clinched. Johnston knew the picture in the locket was of the kid's sister, but this was the Captain's idea of a joke. It didn't strike me as funny. I stood up, took one step forward, and hit him in the face with my fist.

The Captain went reeling back. Coffee spilled down the front of his dirty homespun and the cup clattered to the ground. He slammed into a peach tree and hung on for a moment, blinking. Finally

11

his sluggish brain started working. "Denfield," he said hoarsely, "you'll be a sorry sonofabitch for that!" and he lunged.

Big Belly Johnston had a reputation for being tough, and he was, but he could be hurt. I stepped to one side and clubbed him savagely on the back of his fat neck as he lunged past, and he fell on his face as though he had been shot. That sudden insane rage that had hit me was gone now. Denfield, I thought savagely, you're a fool! A goddamn fool! Here I was in the middle of a fist fight because some fat-bellied captain had made an off-color remark about a photograph.

Johnston, slightly stunned but shaking it off, was getting to his knees. I glanced at the kid and was vaguely surprised to see that he was doing nothing. He was still on one knee, looking on with intense interest, and it seemed to me that he was even smiling slightly. But I must have been mistaken about that. There was no time to wonder about it, for Big Belly was on his feet now, coming at me with both hamlike fists flying.

The noise we were making had drawn something of a crowd by now. They ganged around the firelighted circle, some few of the men in my outfit shouting pieces of advice to me, but most of them doing nothing. I took one of Big Belly's fists in the gut and a great, hot sickness shot into my throat. I was glad enough to hear the hysterical, high-pitched voice of our boy major.

"Gentlemen, gentlemen, we can't forget that we are officers! What kind of example is this to be setting for the men?" The war would never be over for the Major. If he lived to be a hundred, in his heart he would still be an officer in the C.S.A. But just the same, I was glad enough that he had appeared and stopped it before the fortunes of battle began to turn.

The Major was so angry that he almost cried. He said that Big Belly and I were under arrest, but it didn't mean a thing, because his power to give us orders came from his rank in an army that had ceased to exist. But the fight was over anyway. Johnston, cursing darkly, tramped back to his own battery, and the men were scattered and sent back to their own squad fires, and after a few minutes the peach orchard was much the same as it had been before.

"That eye of yours won't be a pretty thing tomorrow," Phil Carney said. He seemed vaguely amused, which didn't do my present mood any good. I had that queasiness inside, the feeling that a man gets when he fully realizes that he has made a complete fool of himself. I wanted to forget the fight and Big Belly Johnston as quickly as possible. The kid opened the whisky bottle and passed it to me.

"I'll bet that's the first fight Big Belly hasn't won in years," he said.

"I'd rather just forget about it."

He shrugged, and for a long while we said nothing. We sat and stared into the fire and drank the whisky, and I don't know what Phil Carney was thinking about, but I was thinking about his sister. A girl I had never even seen. But I couldn't get her out of my mind.

After a while Phil Carney said, "Did I ever tell you about my father, Jeff?" He seemed to have put the fight from his mind. If he thought I had made a fool of myself, at least he was decent enough to keep quiet about it and change the subject.

I said, "What about your father?"

"I never told you about this part of our family history," he said with strange flatness, "but I've been thinkin' about it a good deal lately. My father's dead."

I knew that, so there didn't seem to be anything to say.

"They found him in an arroyo with one side of his head blown off by a forty-four bullet. The pistol was still in his hand."

I was suddenly unable to make a sound. I had never guessed that the kid had ever had any close contact with tragedy—except the war, of course, and that was mostly an impersonal thing. "At the time," he went on with that same flatness, "I had already signed on with the Confederacy. My company was already marchin' toward Arkansas, and by the time I got Laura's letter, I was in Virginia." He turned toward me. "You know, it's a

14

wonder I ever took up with you, Jeff. I've got good cause to hate professional gamblers. The best cause in the world. It was a professional gambler that caused my father's death."

All thought of Big Belly Johnston and the fight left me. Phil Carney had tapped a bitterness within himself that I hadn't known was there. I said, "But I thought . . ."

"That my father killed himself?" He sat stiffly, staring into the fire. "It's all in the way you look at it, I guess. You remember our ranch that I've told you about?" I remembered it well, for he had talked about it often. He set great store by that ranch. "It was the best spread around Sabina," he went on, and his voice was tough. "The best spread in southwest Texas, for that matter. The Carney ranch, that's all the name it had. The brand was a block C. I love that ranch, Jeff. And so does Laura." Then he added, "But it isn't ours now. My father lost it to a gambler."

That was about all there was to the story. Old Man Carney had been roped into a poker game and had lost in a night everything he had worked a lifetime to build, and later, in the darkness of depression, he had killed himself. I had heard the story before. Old-timers told such a story in almost every town along the river where professional gamblers gathered. It was not the kind of thing to make a man proud of his profession. Still, I could not raise much sympathy for Phil

Carney's father. A man had to be weak to take such a way out. And he couldn't have been very smart, for a smart man never gambles with professionals—not even the honest ones.

There was only one thing that made this story slightly different from the others, and that was the intense love that Phil Carney still held for the lost ranch.

"I haven't allowed myself to think about it," Carney said, staring straight ahead. "As long as the war went on, I never knew if I'd see Texas again. But it's over now, so they say. And there seems to be only one thing for me to do now."

"What's that?" I asked after a moment.

"Kill myself a gambler."

This was no harebrained kid talking now. It was a man who had considered all angles of a tough question and had finally come up with the only answer that was right for him. I could feel that he would not be talked out of it, but still I tried.

"Going gunning after a gambler would be suicide," I said. "Sooner or later, in every gambler's life, he knows that he will have to back up a hand with something stronger than cards. A professional gambler must also be the equal of a professional gunman. His trade demands it. You'd be no match for a man like that."

"I've had three years to think about it. There's no other way."

"Is getting yourself killed a solution to anything?"

"My father was cheated out of his ranch," he said stubbornly. "Cheated out of his life."

"Did you see any cheating?" I insisted.

"I didn't see the game. But Laura writes that it's the talk of Sabina."

It was useless to talk, but what else was there to do? He had fought bravely through the war, but he had lived. I could see him now, throwing his life away against a professional gunman, and the thought made me cold.

Then, the words coming slowly, he said, "Maybe there is another way." And I began to breathe easier. "But," he added, "that will be up to you, I guess."

"How's that?"

"I've seen a lot of dead men, but I never saw one cry out in anger, or pain, or for any other reason. You can't hurt them. I don't like to think of this gambler being in a position where I couldn't hurt him. To hurt and keep hurting a man like that, I think you'd have to work on his pride. Rob him of what he holds valuable. To hurt this man, I figure he would have to be beat at gamblin'."

That was the moment when I began to understand that a kind of trap was being laid for me. But I knew it was there and I didn't have to step into it. But I did.

I said, "How do I fit in? I couldn't promise to

17

take another gambler at his own game, if that's what you have in mind."

"I'm not askin' you to fight my fights for me."

"I know you better than that," I said.

But did I? After a long silence, he said, "It was just an idea. Forget it. But if you go back to the river, you'll need a stake, won't you? I've got a little money put by for me in Sabina. You can have it."

"I don't want your money," I said, half in anger. "I just don't think I could help you."

I thought I saw him smile, but it must have been firelight and shadows playing tricks with my eyes. He dropped the subject completely and we spread our blankets for the night. I felt of my jaw and it was sore and beginning to swell. Goddamn that Big Belly Johnston! I thought. But Johnston had little to do with the way I felt, for it was myself that I was angry with. From here on Phil Carney could protect his sister's name if it needed protecting. It was none of my affair.

Or so I told myself. I set my mind to forgetting the whole business. I lay back on the ground, thinking how still the night seemed without cannon or musketry. No more grapeshot or canister, no more hills to charge, no more bloody retreats. The battalion—what was left of it—had camped that night in a peach orchard, cold and bare in the early spring. The Confederacy was no more, they said. Soon the men would start their long walks back to Alabama and Arkansas and Louisiana and try to pick up the frayed-out ends of their old lives. Some of them, like Phil Carney, were only beginning to fight.

How could I have known the kid so long and learned so little about him?

Thinking back on it, I began to remember things that hadn't seemed significant at the time. His unexpected bursts of laughter seemed, as I recalled the times, to ring faintly hollow. And was that eternal grin of his really a grin at all? Or was it a mask? And I remembered the savageness with which he had fought. His brawlings in Richmond taverns. The abrupt disillusionment of susceptible young women who had tried to mother him. All those things made up a part of Phil Carney that I liked, for most of the traits were my traits as well as his. Now I wondered if the kid I knew was really Phil Carney, or an actor who would return to his normal self the moment the curtain fell.

It looked as though the curtain had fallen.

Still, there was Laura. The girl of the letters— the girl of the locket. What was the real Laura like? I wondered. It was a thought that was never far away from my mind.

Forget her. That's the smartest thing to do.

But when I shut her out of my mind, there was only emptiness to take her place.

We lay by the dying fire, Phil Carney and I, wrapped in our war-dirty blankets, and somewhere in the distance we could hear drunken laughter. Another Johnny Reb, it seemed, had visited the Yankee sutler. But most of the men were silent. In the dancing light of a hundred small squad fires, I could see them moving heavily through the peach orchard, some of them already headed home, without waiting for the formalities of pardons. Yesterday they had called it deserting, but there had been just as many.

Then, breaking in on my aimless thoughts, Phil Carney rolled over in his blanket and said, "I'll see you tomorrow."

"Sure."

"By the way, my sister would be glad to see you, if you decide to come with me. I've told her a great deal about you in my letters."

I had nothing to say to that. It appeared that Phil Carney had known all along about that little dream of mine.

Chapter Two

In that cold April of 1865 we left Virginia. Some few of the cavalrymen left on horses, some got rides on freight wagons heading west, but most of us walked. Phil Carney and I walked as far as Petersburg—the city coming slowly to life after the winter siege—and then we became lucky and caught a tinker's hack to Norfolk.

In Norfolk we signed on with a stern-wheeler cotton freighter headed down the coast to Fort Houston, and that was how we got to Texas. Already we were beginning to see what the war had done to the South. Norfolk was a ghost town, Charleston stood stunned and empty-eyed; in New Orleans the children asked for food. We heard stories of treasury agents and carpetbaggers and military government. Old men with angry eyes watched at the docks as we loaded the cotton. "We ought to of throwed in with Johnson. We never ought to of quit fightin'." But the war was history now, and we were going to Texas. To a town I had never even heard of until three years before, a place called Sabina. Exactly why, I couldn't have said.

Friendship? Probably not, for war friendships were affairs of circumstance; and besides, Phil Carney was a different man from the one I thought I had known. Still, I liked the kid as well as I had ever liked anyone, and I had a great deal of respect for his fighting ability and bravery, although most of the time his bravery was senseless. I couldn't count friendship out altogether.

Probably it was a combination of things that finally decided me. Curiosity played a part. And a genuine concern about what would happen when Carney's incredible string of luck finally played out, as it was bound to someday. Too, I wanted to see this gambler who had started everything. I felt that if I could talk to him, or maybe get together with him over a hand of poker, I would somehow know if he was capable of cheating a man out of his home.

But the most important thing was Laura, the kid's sister. The situation was senseless, and I knew it, and that still didn't change things. There is no explaining the way an aimless thought can become lodged in a man's mind, living there and growing until it becomes an obsession. Look, I told myself, why don't you just forget her? But it wasn't that easy. Over the three years of war I had built in my mind a woman of absolute perfection, and her name was Laura Carney. From four principal sources I had gathered the material for my creation:

Her letters to her brother, for one. From this source came the qualities of gentleness and dignity and an admirable self-sufficiency. After her father's death and the loss of the ranch she had moved to Sabina and taken over the operation of a boardinghouse and had made it pay. From what I had heard of her letters, she didn't seem as bitter as her brother about what had happened— although I had guessed by now that the kid had skipped that part when he read the letters aloud.

A more prolific source of material had been the long talks that I had had with Phil Carney. Between campaigns, between battles. Time goes slowly in the army, and talk is free. From these talks I had learned much about the Carney family—the mother who had died giving birth to Phil, the father who drank too much and gambled too much, but who had a fine mind for business and cattle. And I learned about the little town of Sabina in southwest Texas, and the Indian reservations in the New Mexico country, where they sold their cattle, and the rustlers who raided across the Rio Grande from Mexico. I learned about wild-cow hunts and brush-poppers and a lot of other things, but much of the time I only pretended to listen until Laura's name was mentioned. Even her name added to the illusion of perfection. Soft-sounding, as a woman's name should be, but with no hint of flimsiness. The name of Carney didn't seem to go with a name like that. I once caught myself thinking, Laura Denfield.

The quality of beauty, of course, came from the locket that Phil Carney always carried with him. The old daguerreotype was scarred and faded, but the beauty of the girl was inescapable.

So those were the sources from which I gathered the material. I assembled the material in my mind and created a woman of incredible beauty and grace and dignity. Unlike God, I had used no imperfect qualities in my creation.

The fact that I finally had to face was that I had to do something about this Galatea of mine. I had created her and it was up to me to destroy her.

Until I did, there would be no satisfaction in women for me, for they would all seem insipid and pale alongside the woman in my mind. Well, I thought, a dream can be destroyed, like anything else. All you have to do is compare it with its counterpart in reality—in this case, Laura Carney. And I guess that is the real reason I took that cotton freighter from Virginia to Texas, when all instincts warned me to stay out of other people's battles.

I remember the day we first sighted Sabina. Since I had been born in Missouri and had lived most of my life in the river country, this was a wild, strange country to me. After leaving the cotton boat in Houston we began a series of long and torturous rides in aged, dilapidated Concord coaches, headed always to the west. As we left the lushness of the lowlands and began crashing into that tangled wilderness of boulders and grease-wood and sage, Phil Carney seemed somehow to gain new life and a brightness came to his eyes. Phil Carney was coming home. For me, it was something else.

The blazing sun acted as a tonic to the kid. For me, it sapped my energy and made me irritable and sweaty and sorry that I had ever listened to my own madness. Reddish dust fogged through the windows of the coach and covered the passengers like stifling shrouds. It clogged my nostrils and dried my throat, and it mixed with sweat and became a gummy, mudlike substance that clung to every exposed inch of my body like the clammy hand of death. So this was the Texas brush country, the land of the Carneys. Over there somewhere, beyond the sea of brush and dagger thorns, was the Big River, and Mexico.

"It's over there," Phil Carney said, pointing through the open coach window. "About an hour away. There's another way stop, though, before we get there."

He was talking about Sabina. He had been talking about it almost constantly for two days now, and I had long since stopped listening. There had not been a recurrence of the mood that had taken hold of him in the peach orchard on that night that now seemed so long ago in Virginia. It seemed that he had once again bottled up his anger and had stowed it away in some dark corner of his mind, and to all appearances he was the same reckless hell-for-leather kid that I had known through three years of war. He did not speak of his father after that night, or of the gambler. Occasionally he mentioned Laura, but mostly it was Sabina that he talked about.

At the way station we picked up fresh horses and a whisky drummer headed for Sabina. The drummer glanced cynically at our filthy, worn-out uniforms. Then, holding his sample case on his lap, he somehow managed to go to sleep.

"What do you think about it?" the kid said.

I looked at him, vaguely amused that a man could take pride in a country like this. "It's not much like the river country."

"I guess not. But you'll come to like it when you get to know it."

I hoped that I wouldn't be here long enough to become intimately acquainted with it, but I didn't say so. Pretty soon we began to see ranch hands along the stage road, headed into Sabina for supplies, or to pick up the mail, or maybe just to have a drink of rotgut and look at a saloon girl. They were tall, awkward men, most of them, their faces as brown as saddle leather, their eyes faded and pale from too much staring into that ever-lasting sun. Some of them still wore parts of battered Confederate uniforms, but most of them wore narrow-brimmed hats and collarless hickory shirts and leather work chaps. All of them had revolvers on their hips, in open holsters. No vest-pocket derringers for these men. Unsmilingly they pulled their horses off the road and raised their hands as the stage jolted past.

"Our ranch is over that way," Phil Carney said, pointing again. He grinned quietly to himself. Apparently he had forgotten that the ranch now belonged to a gambler.

It was late in the afternoon when the coach finally rattled into Sabina, with a great deal of noise and show, the way stagecoaches always enter a town. It was about an hour before dark and the die-hard sun still blazed savagely in the west when I got my first look at the kid's home town.

There wasn't much to it, and certainly there was nothing special about it that I could see. There was just one street, a dusty, deep-rutted affair, flanked on both sides by sagging frame buildings. The wagon yard and corral set a short distance away from the town, and we could smell it several minutes before we reached it. The coach rattled and jolted to a stop in front of the stage office, which was also a general store, and the driver climbed down from his box, and began getting our rolls out of the boot.

Five or six town loafers had been waiting for the stage, and now they came forward to see who, if anybody, would get off. "Sabina's official reception committee." The kid grinned.

"So I guessed."

The whisky drummer was the first to get off. Then the kid swung out and one of the old men came forward, squinting. "Dang me if it ain't Matt Carney's boy!"

"That's right, Sandy." The kid grinned, shaking the old man's hand.

"Figured maybe the Yankees'd got you."

"Not this time, old-timer." Carney shook hands all around, answering questions and grinning. How much of the grin was real, I had no way of knowing. He said, "Is my sister still at the Charleston House?"

"Figure she is," another oldster put in. "Didn't know you was comin', I guess."

"I guess not. By the way, this is Captain Jefferson Denfield."

"Pleased to make your acquaintance," said the old man called Sandy. "What part of Texas you from, Cap'n?"

"Didn't come from Texas at all, old-timer," the kid said. And the old man blinked, as though such a thing were unheard of. "Look," Carney said, "we'd better get out of here, Jeff. Sandy'll talk your leg off if you let him."

"You aim to stay a spell in Sabina, Cap'n?" Sandy asked.

"You might call it a visit," I said. "No, I don't plan to stay long."

The driver got our baggage down—our blanket rolls, the only baggage we had. We picked them up and made our way through the tobacco-chewing, stick-whittling old men and started up the street away from the stage office. My insides felt hollow. A sickness began rising in my throat and I knew what that meant. It meant that I was scared.

Eyes were watching us as we tramped up the dusty street. Men stopped Phil Carney and shook his hand and asked brief questions about the war, and they looked at me and wondered what I was doing in a place like Sabina. But all I could think was: This is the place where Laura lives.

28

I suddenly wanted to get back on the coach and get as far away as the Butterfield line would take me. But the stage was already pulling out. This is the cure you prescribed for yourself, I thought. You might as well see it through.

We passed a barbershop and I said, "Look, why don't you go on and see your sister and I'll stay behind and clean up a little. Tell me where the place is and I'll come around later." But the way I looked didn't bother me so much. I was simply trying to postpone the exploding of a dream.

Carney laughed. "You can clean up when we get to the Charleston House."

"I'm not exactly in any condition to be introduced to a lady."

"Laura? She's just my sister."

There was no talking myself out of it. I tried to think of something else. I put my attention on the town itself, as we walked through it, and after a while it began to come to me that there was something here that I hadn't noticed before, something that made the town different from others we had seen in the South. At first I had trouble deciding what it was, for there was nothing about the weather-scabbed, false-fronted buildings or the deep-rutted street to set it apart from other towns. Finally I discovered that it was the people who were different. I couldn't put my finger on the word to describe them or the thing that made them different; it was something in their eyes, in the way they walked, in the heartiness of their greetings, in the clothes they wore. And then I knew what it was. I knew the word to describe them. Prosperous.

It had been a long while since I had seen a prosperous Southerner, but that's what these people were. Then at last I remembered where we were: Sabina, tucked securely away in this God-forgotten corner of Texas, almost in Mexico, where the war couldn't get at it the way it had done in the other towns and communities of the South. The foragers, both Yankee and Rebel, had missed Sabina in their plunderings. Here homes and property had remained safe, the market for their cattle secure in the Indian reservations to the west.

I stopped for a moment, unable to believe that there was a town in the South that war had not touched with its withering hand. But there was such a town, and it was Sabina. The country all around it had fallen victim to the crawling death; Sabina had grown robust. If it had not been for the conspicuous scarcity of young men, the silent young men who had ridden away to strange lands to do their fighting and dying for the Confederacy, you would not believe that there had been a war at all.

"What's the matter?" I heard Phil Carney saying.

"Nothing. I was just thinking about this town of yours."

We were soon past the main string of business buildings—the harness shops, feed stores, general stores, saloons—all of them well stocked, as far as I could see. At the end of the street there was a big two-story frame building with a big pillared porch in front, and in front of the porch was a faded plank sign: "Charleston House—Room and Board—Meals 75c a Day." After the "75c" an afterthought had been added: "Hard Money." And that was the Charleston House, the place where she lived and worked.

I tried to think objectively about it as we walked toward it. It had been a pretty fancy place at one time. A few years back it had been white, but the sun and weather had peeled the paint away in huge patches, and now it was no color at all that you could name. There were two wicker chairs and two rockers on the front porch, and at the side of the house there was a long wash bench for the boarders who wanted to clean up before eating. Two men who looked like visiting cow hands sat on the end of the porch, talking away time while the evening meal was being put on the table.

We stopped for a moment before the sagging picket fence in front of the house, shifting our blanket rolls. Carney looked at me and shrugged, which meant nothing in particular. He wasn't grinning now, I noticed.

He kicked open the gate and we went up the dirt path to the front porch. The two cow hands didn't bother to look around. The front door stood open, so we walked into what was once a front parlor but was now an almost vacant room. The smell of cooking food hit us and my stomach began to shrink, and I realized that it had been almost twelve hours since I had eaten.

We stood for a moment in the center of the bare room, still holding our blanket rolls, both of us a bit uncomfortable. Off in another room there was the rattle of pans and dishes. "Well, by God," the kid said, "Jeb Stuart could bring a regiment of cavalry through here and nobody'd know the difference." Then he shouted: "Laura!"

A voice came from the other room. "Who is it?" I felt a swelling ache in my chest and realized that I had been holding my breath. Then, suddenly I was looking at her.

She stood in the doorway, wiping her hands on an apron, her eyes wide and slightly startled as all three of us stood there saying nothing. It's not the girl in the picture! I thought. It can't be! At last, with very little emotion in his voice, Phil Carney said, "Hello, Laura," and dropped his roll to the floor.

She was not the girl in the picture. I knew that. She was rather tall and her neck was longer and her shoulders were wider than most girls', and that was all I noticed. I looked down at the floor. Well, there goes your dream, Denfield!

A cloud of dust billowed up where he dropped

the roll, and Phil Carney said, "Let me look at you. You haven't changed much, Laura." He walked over to her and stood in front of her, grinning thinly.

Then she spoke for the first time. "I told you not to come back here." There was anger in her eyes.

"This is a fine reception," her brother said dryly.

"I *told* you not to come back," she said again.

"I don't always do what I'm told, Laura, although I've improved some with three years of war. I almost forgot; this is Captain Denfield. I wrote you about him."

She didn't look at me or even acknowledge that I was in the room. Still looking at her brother, she said, "Phil, you've got to get out of Sabina."

The kid shrugged, the grin a frozen thing on his face. "Is it all right if we eat supper first?" he asked flatly. "That wouldn't put you out too much, would it?"

Her eyes struck fire. "You know what I mean!"

"Jeff," the kid said over his shoulder, "this is my sister, Laura." When she still said nothing and still didn't look at me, he added, "The whole South has changed, hasn't it, Jeff? Things are never the way you expect them to be."

"The Army didn't improve your manners," she said.

"Speaking of manners . . ." The kid shrugged again, holding onto that stiff grin. "Are we invited to supper?"

33

"When will you leave Sabina?"

"She's got a one-track mind," Phil Carney said to me. "Maybe I didn't mention that when I told you about her."

"Phil, answer me!"

"I don't plan to *ever* leave Sabina!" he almost shouted. Then his voice dropped abruptly to normal. "Where's Old Lady Lorring?"

She stood like a statue while the kid looked at her with that frozen grin. Abruptly he turned and walked into the other room—the dining room, I guessed—and I heard him calling, "Mrs. Lorrin'! Mrs. Lorrin'!"

As from a great distance, I could hear Phil's heavy infantry boots tramping through the house, and I stood there in the center of the room, uncomfortable and sweating, wondering if I should say something. But what was there to say? Damn that kid, I thought. Goddamn him for ever bringing me to this God-forsaken edge of nowhere!

Laura Carney was still standing exactly the way she had been when I first saw her, staring straight ahead, as though her brother were still there. She was a complete stranger to me. She was nothing like the fanciful picture of perfection that I had been carrying around in my mind, and she only faintly resembled the picture in the locket.

I stared at her now and she didn't seem to mind, didn't even seem to know that I was in the room.

Her eyes, I noticed, were dark and wide-set and angry. Her hair was dark brown, and she didn't wear it in the elaborate, over-the-ears dovetail fashion of the day, but had it pulled severely back behind her ears and done up in a tidy little bun at the nape of her neck. She wore a gray and white cotton house dress, and an overall apron, somewhat faded and worn from too many washings and ironings. She was no beauty. She certainly couldn't compare to my own personally created Galatea, but there was a cleanness and straightness about her that was easy to admire. When she was angry, as she was now, it showed in every move she made, in every flick of an eyelash. It would be very difficult to lie to a girl like that, I thought. She looked extremely competent and firm and reliable, and, without a great strain on the imagination, she might be called pretty. But she wasn't the girl in the locket or my mind, and I felt cheated.

Well, I thought, you asked for it. This is the reason you came to Sabina, isn't it? To explode a dream?

The heavy tramp of the kid's boots came back through the house, and he came into the room with a fat woman on his arm.

"Mrs. Lorrin', this is the man I was tellin' you about, Captain Denfield."

"*Captain* Denfield!" The fat woman beamed. "My, yes, I remember. Welcome to Sabina, Captain."

"Just 'mister' now," I said. "But thanks."

Mrs. Lorring was almost a caricature of a fat woman, round cheeks, trembling chins, eyes that were bright and alive. She looked breathless and flushed, and it was obvious that Phil had been teasing her. Phil had a way with a woman when he found one that he liked. That wasn't often. Smiling so wide that the corners of her mouth pushed her cheeks up and almost closed her eyes in folds of fat, Mrs. Lorring turned to Laura Carney.

"My, Laury, ain't you thrilled to have this young devil back home?"

I could see Laura getting a hold on herself as she forced a smile. Phil did something that I didn't see, and Mrs. Lorring screamed and burst into a shattering stream of giggling. "Do we get a room?" He grinned.

"Of course," she said, composing herself. "Laury, you get things on the table and I'll—" And she broke off in another burst of giggling. "Phil, you don't change none at all!"

"The room," he reminded her.

"I *said* you could have one!"

"And a bath. Two baths. As soon as it gets dark, will you put on some water to heat?"

"You look like you need one. My!"

The chatter kept up as the kid picked up his blanket roll and the two of us followed Mrs. Lorring out of the room and up a flight of stairs, leaving Laura in that same rigid position, staring and angry. When is the next stage east? I wondered. I'd already had enough of Sabina. And the dream was dead; it couldn't be deader.

The room we got was a large one, and one of Mrs. Lorring's best. There were two iron beds and a big mahogany dresser with a marble top and two armless, high-backed rockers. About the kind of room that you would expect to find in a place like the Charleston House, in a town like Sabina, Texas, in the year 1865.

I began untying my roll when the landlady left us alone. "You and Mrs. Lorring seem to get along," I said. I didn't want to talk about Laura. The less I thought of her, the better.

"I've known the old lady since I was a kid," Phil said, breaking his own blanket open. "She used to run the academy here in Sabina. My father sent me to school there. Then she got married and her husband was a cattle buyer, and we used to see quite a bit of them. A wild cow killed Old Man Lorrin' about two years before the war, so the old lady bought this place to live on."

That seemed to take care of Mrs. Lorring, owner of the Charleston House. I felt dirty and gritty and worn out, and still uncomfortable from the scene that had taken place in the parlor. Sitting on the bed, I scattered the contents of my roll, the sum total of Jefferson Denfield's assets. Among the odds and ends there were a blue hickory shirt, a pair of homespun trousers that I had bought in Richmond almost two years ago, a razor and strap, and a brass-framed Griswold and Grier .36-caliber revolver, complete with C.S.A. holster and belt. The revolver was still loaded with the same rounds that had been in it the day of the surrender.

I left the shirt and trousers on the bed and started to put the revolver back, and the kid said, "Keep it out."

I looked at him and he was inspecting his own revolver, a Spiller and Burr copy of the Colt, exactly like mine except that his had a seven-inch barrel. He said, "Keep it out and wear it. You don't need a pistol often in Sabina, but when you do, you need it bad."

Was this his way of telling me something? I almost said that I wouldn't be staying in Sabina long enough to keep the gun out, but I felt too empty to argue, so I put the revolver on the bed. For a while I thought that he wasn't going to say anything about his sister, and I was hoping he wouldn't. But then he lay across the bed, putting his dirty boots on the iron bedstead, and said:

"I guess you've been wonderin' what kind of family this is. The Carneys, I mean."

I couldn't think of any answer to that.

He lay there grinning, that same fixed grin that I had seen earlier. "I have," he said, after a long pause. "I've been doin' a little wonderin' about me, too. Jeff, do you want me to tell you somethin'?"

"If you want to." All I wanted was a bath, some clean clothes, and a ticket on the next stage out of Sabina.

"It's about me. And it's not pretty."

"Then don't tell it."

He lay there for more than a minute before he spoke again.

"That ranch my father lost," he said at last. "I want that ranch more than I ever wanted anything in my life, and I guess there's nothin' I wouldn't do to get it. I'll take it from Jay McCain, too, or I'll die tryin'."

McCain was the gambler, and it was the first time Carney had mentioned him in more than a month. There didn't seem to be anything for me to say, so I sat there and waited for him to go on.

"What did you think of my sister?" he asked abruptly.

To give my hands something to do, I picked up my revolver and bounced it lightly from one hand to the other. "She's an attractive girl."

He laughed harshly. "But not as attractive as you thought she'd be, is she?" Lying on his back, he turned his head slightly and glanced at me. "I know why you came to Sabina, Jeff. It wasn't because of me, or my father, or the ranch. It was because of Laura, wasn't it?"

Denying it would do no good. I said nothing.

"Forget her," he said flatly, looking back at the ceiling. "You've probably guessed by now that I began planning a long time ago for you to come to Sabina with me. That's why I talked about Laura so much. I knew it would take more than army friendship to bring you down here to a place that you didn't know, so I gave you my sister." He laughed suddenly, harshly. "Most of the things I told you were lies. Most of the things I read from her letters were lies, too, but I guess you know that now." He paused, then went on. "The picture in the locket, of course, was of my mother, when she was a girl. She was the only beauty the Carney family ever had."

Too stunned to say anything, I sat there for a long moment, my hands automatically pitching the revolver back and forth. For another person the situation could have been amusing, but my sense of humor seemed to have gone sour, and I felt only anger at myself. Jeff Denfield, professional gambler, I thought, being drawn into the most brazen sucker play of them all! I said finally:

"Is that all you wanted to tell me?"

"Not quite." And he paused for a moment, as though he didn't exactly know how to say the rest of it. "You're probably mad now," he said, not looking at me. "I can't say that I blame you."

"Tell me one thing," I said tightly. "Tell me why you went to all this trouble."

"I want you to get my ranch from Jay McCain,"

he said calmly. When I stood up, he swung around to a sitting position and said, "Just a minute, Jeff, before you go off the handle. This is kind of a long story and I don't know just how to get it started."

"Just for once," I said angrily, "why don't you start by telling the truth? Just for the hell of it. That ought to be a great novelty."

"All right." In his roll he had found a small bundle of dried and ragged cigars. He handed one to me, then took one for himself and began licking it into shape. "All right," he said again, "we'll start with the truth. We'll go all the way back to the time when they found my father in the gully with his brains blown out. Well, they found him in the gully, all right, but not the way I told it. He had been thrown from his horse, and when he hit the ground his neck was broken."

Calmly Phil Carney found a sulphur match and held it for me to light my cigar. Then he lit his own and walked over to the window, looking down on Sabina. "And that's the truth about the way my father died," he said. "That was about four years ago, and the ranch was still ours then. Or mine. My father left the place to me."

I didn't get the implication at first. Then it fell on me like cold water. "*You're* the one that lost the ranch to McCain?"

"Yes."

The sheer weight of so much lying left me

numb. Lies had given birth to that outlandish dream, lies had formed a friendship, and finally lies had brought me almost two thousand miles to this barren wilderness that they called Sabina. I was past anger. There was only a biting bitterness somewhere inside me as I said:

"I want to know one thing. Why didn't you tell me the truth to start with?"

"The truth wouldn't have brought you here." Still looking out of the window, he said, "Not even our friendship or the lie about my father would have brought you, and that was the reason I used Laura. That was the cruelest thing, I guess, for you're not the only man in the war who got through mostly on hope of some kind. My hope was for the ranch. Yours was for a woman that never existed, and never could exist." He laughed shortly. "The woman I helped you build in your mind sure wasn't my sister, anyway."

Goddamn him! I thought. If I had let myself, I think I could have killed him.

He turned from the window then. Dusk was falling over Sabina and it was getting dark in the room. Outside we could hear boots scraping on the front porch and the quiet sound of men talking. It was near suppertime and the boarders were beginning to gather. Phil Carney said, "I've done so much lyin' that maybe you won't believe me now. But you're the closest thing to a friend I ever had, Jeff. We saw a lot together with Hood and the others. Can't we keep it going, the way it was then?"

My anger flared like bomb powder, and was gone almost immediately. "It's no good." I shook my head.

"You haven't heard my proposition yet. The big problem was getting you to Sabina. If I could do that, I knew you'd help me. All I ask is that you see Jay McCain and talk to him, and then if you still don't want to help me, I'll buy you a stage ticket to St. Louis."

"No."

"Look." His voice was edged with urgency. "Jeff, I don't blame you for being mad, but all I told you back in Virginia wasn't a lie. The part about the cheating is true. He cheated me out of my ranch. There's no way I can prove it, but I know it just the same. All I ask is that you watch him play—and then if you don't think he's capable of cheating, I'll still buy that stage ticket."

"Even if I was fool enough to listen to you," I said, "even if I hated this gambler's guts, what could I do?"

He said evenly, "You could win my ranch back."

I knew what he was going to say, and that was what he had been planning for three years. The knowledge was staggering. For three years he had cultivated my friendship, had planted the seed of an insane dream in my mind, had somehow persuaded me to travel halfway across the continent, and all for one single purpose—to get me to win back a ranch that he had so stupidly lost. As though it were as easy as that. Taking a few dollars from a backwoods farmer or saloon idler was one thing, but taking money from a professional gambler was something entirely different. Even if I had wanted to try it, it would have been impossible. I had no stake. I had no reason to believe that this Jay McCain wasn't as good a gambler as I was or better. And if he was a second-card artist, as Carney seemed to think, that made it all the more difficult.

I stood up and began tying my blanket roll.

"What are you doing?"

"I'm catching the next coach out of Sabina. In the meantime, I'll find another place to stay."

"Jeff, you haven't heard my proposition!" The words came fast now. "Look, I'll pay you. I have two thousand dollars that my father put away for me until I was of age. You can use that for a stake."

"I'm not interested."

"Listen to me! All I want is my ranch back. Any money you win over that you can keep."

Suddenly I wanted to laugh. All he wanted was a five-thousand-acre ranch, fully stocked, no doubt, and making money on its own! A gambler could work a lifetime and never make a killing like that. Still, in the back of my mind I had the feeling that there was more to it than the ranch alone. The situation was too urgent, the means too desperate for the end.

But that was none of my business. I shouldered the roll and turned for the door. "Well, I guess this is good-by, kid."

He said nothing. He looked very young at that moment, and completely defeated. And, for some reason, I said, "Is there anything else?"

He took a deep drag on his frayed cigar, and I could imagine that I saw him shrinking as he exhaled the bluish smoke. "There's just one thing I haven't told you," he said flatly. "Laura aims to marry Jay McCain."

Chapter Three

Several seconds must have passed with neither of us making a sound. Downstairs we heard dishes rattling. Supper was on the table.

I don't know why it jarred me to hear that Laura was marrying the gambler. I don't see how anything could have surprised me at that point. But it did.

"All right," I said wearily, "I might as well hear the rest of it." I knew at the time that it was the wrong thing to say, but Laura Carney marrying a gambler just didn't make sense. I didn't put my roll down. Even then I had hopes of getting out of Sabina. I wanted the easygoing, slow-moving atmosphere of the river country as I had never wanted anything before. I wanted to feel the sluggish roll of a river boat, and relax at a felt-top table with men that I knew and understood. But something held me. Something made me invite the kid to go on; it made about as much sense as taking two cards to a flush and raising.

Soberly now, Phil Carney said, "I guess you know by now that Laura and I don't agree on everything that comes up. We've been fightin' since we were kids, and we'll go on fightin', I guess, because that's the way people grow up in this country. We fight hard and argue hard, and most of it, probably, is to cover up the way we really feel. You'll understand that if you see McCain. She's marryin' him so I can get the ranch back." He paused for a moment, his eyes bright. "I guessed it was somethin' like that, when she kept writin' me not to worry. When I accused her of it . . ." He spread his hands. "Well, that's the way it was."

There were things about the Carneys that I still didn't understand. "I don't get it. How could Laura's marrying McCain get the ranch back for *you?*"

He laughed shortly. "You underestimate Laura's gift for planning. When she agreed to marry McCain, it was on the condition that he would sell the ranch back to me, taking the two thousand dollars down and letting me pay the rest out as I could."

It was still incredible to me, everything about it. If the ranch was so valuable, I couldn't see a man like McCain agreeing to give it up. And I couldn't see a girl like Laura marrying a man she hated for the lone purpose of acquiring a piece of Texas real estate.

Phil smiled thinly and seemed to read my mind. "Why would McCain agree to play when he knows the deck is stacked? If you lived in this country, you'd understand. Down here, the Carney name stands for power, respectability, permanence—in spite of what I've done to it. Maybe McCain loves my sister, but that isn't the important thing. It's the name he wants, and the respectability that would go with marrying a Carney. Anyway, McCain's no rancher. He still spends most of his time in town." Then, changing directions abruptly, he said, "I guess you don't know what a ranch is like, especially down here in the brush country, do you?"

I stood dumbly, not understanding what this had to do with his sister. "A brush ranch isn't much to look at," he said, "even the big ones. They're not like the big spreads up north on the Brazos, or in the Panhandle. This is hard country down here, and it takes a big man to get the best out of it—but when he does, he knows that he's done somethin'. My father was like that. He came down here when there was nothing but Mexicans and mesquite and wild cows, and almost singlehanded he built one of the biggest outfits south of the Pecos. During the Mexican war he fought for the land, and after the war he beat the brush and rounded up wild cows as mean as tigers, and he built barns and corrals and shacks, and after a while he had the beginning of a ranch. All the hard part he did himself, but later I had a hand in it too. And so did Laura, for that matter. We helped build because we knew that it was to be ours someday."

He stood up. "And then one night I rode into town and got drunk and lost it. In one night I lost what it had taken my father a lifetime to build. Are you beginning to understand that there's nothin' I would stop at to get it back?"

It was one of the longest speeches I had ever heard him make. He didn't look much like a kid now. "Unless you know what it is to tear a living from land like this," he went on, "you can't understand how much a brush ranch can mean to a man. Laura knows. She's a woman and she hasn't got the same feel for land that a man has, but still she knows what it means to me."

I felt uncomfortable now, as though I had been caught eavesdropping on an intimate family discussion. I said finally, "And that's the only reason she intends to marry McCain?"

"See McCain and decide for yourself."

He took a few steps forward and stood looking at me. "I guess this is all I've got to say, Jeff."

He could have said more. He could have told

me that, if nothing else happened to stop the marriage, he would go gunning for McCain. That way, no matter who got killed, the necessity for Laura's marrying the gambler would be removed. Or he could have explained further the reason for all the lies that had brought me to Sabina. But he didn't. He merely looked at me, with the barest trace of an iron-hard grin.

Finally he exhaled loudly, as though he had been holding his breath. "I'm sorry, Jeff," he said with a hint of a shrug. "No hard feelings?"

"No."

"The stage that brought us in will be headin' east again tomorrow. I'm still good for that stage ticket."

"I'll manage."

"Well, take care of yourself."

"Sure."

And still I stood there, feeling a fool with that roll on my shoulder. I don't remember just what crazy thoughts were going through my mind at that moment. Maybe I was remembering the time at Bloody Angle when I got the Minie ball in the thigh. Maybe I was seeing the kid fighting his way through a nightmare of grapeshot and musketry to drag me into a ditch. Possibly I remembered the brawling drunks we had been on together in Richmond and other places. Or those long, aching marches up and down the Shenandoah Valley, the men cursing and bleeding, and the stragglers falling farther and farther behind; and then, because a wild-eyed kid with a brazen grin came loping toward you, the war seemed less miserable.

It could have been any of those things, and many more. But later, looking back on it, I had the uneasy feeling that it had been something altogether different. A locket, some letters, a thousand lies, and my imagination. . . .

I threw the roll on the bed and said, "Oh, hell!"

Then his face loosened and he really grinned. I knew that he was going to, and I had a savage impulse to hit him. What I did was untie my roll again and say:

"Do you think we can have those baths now?"

So that was how I came to stay in Sabina; not for any one reason, but for a lot of small reasons, some of them so insignificant that they seemed no excuses at all. The decision didn't improve my mood, and the kid, sensing that, kept his mouth shut and went downstairs to see about hot water for the baths.

We bathed in darkness, in two wooden tubs placed behind the smokehouse behind the Charleston House. A Negro handy man brought kettles of hot water and flour-sack towels and yellow homemade soap, and we scrubbed and scratched and clawed the crust of desert filth from our bodies. As we stood naked and shivering in the tubs behind the smokehouse, I thought that there were still many questions that needed to be answered, but at that particular time I had my fill of the Carney family and its troubles. Apparently the kid had got around to telling the truth at last, and that was something. If I could help him— well, maybe I owed him that much from the war. I made a careful point of not thinking of Laura Carney at all. Oh, there's nothing like an exploded dream, I thought wryly, to set a man on the right track!

After we were bathed and dressed, there were only our worn Confederate Army boots and campaign hats to remind us of the war that had already passed into history. The kid, like myself, had discarded his tattered uniform in favor of hickory and homespun. Like the other citizens of Sabina, we began to ignore the uneasy rumblings of further trouble drifting down from northern Texas. Talk of state police, and the bluebelly government, and treasury agents. Such Reconstruction trouble was not apt to reach so remote a place as Sabina, except indirectly. I was glad of that, for there was apt to be enough trouble as it was.

Phil Carney was remarkably silent throughout the bathing and dressing. I sensed that his attitude had changed. Short of a shoot-out with McCain, he had done everything possible, and now it was up to me.

Up to me to do what? Regain a ranch that he had stupidly thrown away? Save his sister from this melodramatic marriage contract that she had bound herself to? Save the kid from getting his fool self killed? I felt like an inadequate god called upon to perform impossible miracles.

Mrs. Lorring, still giggling and beaming upon Phil Carney, fed us turnip greens and side meat in the kitchen after the paying boarders had finished in the dining room. Laura was nowhere to be seen. After we had eaten, I went upstairs and the kid followed. As I buckled on the revolver, he sat on the bed, rolling a cigar in his mouth.

"I think I'll have a look at Sabina," I said. "If you don't mind, I'll go by myself."

"Thanks." Staring at his cigar, the word got stuck and he had to clear his throat. "Thanks for not leaving, Jeff."

"Don't thank me until I've done something. The odds are a thousand to one that I'll accomplish nothing, even if I decide to try. You know that, don't you?"

He nodded, still giving careful attention to the cigar. Then, when I turned for the door, he said, "Good luck," and I went out.

The empty parlor was dark and seemed even emptier than before. There was the sound of dishes being washed in the kitchen, and the yellowish light of a coal-oil lamp slanted through the dining-room doorway as I went out to the front porch. I stood on the porch for a moment, breathing in the coolness of the night, which seemed almost refreshing after the blazing heat of a few hours ago. The porch seemed deserted. There was the sweetish, heavy smell of honeysuckle on the sluggish air. As I started to step down to the dirt walk, a voice said:

"Cap'n Denfield?"

He came around from the end of the porch where he had been standing, and I saw that it was the old man called Sandy, one of the group that had met us at the stage office. He shuffled forward, chewing, spitting, squinting in the darkness. "The boy ain't with you?"

"Phil? He's upstairs, I think. Why?"

He rubbed his chin, still squinting up at me. "I was just wonderin'," he said finally. "Old Matt Carney was well liked in these parts. We like the boy, too, even if he does get a mite wild at times. The thing is, we wouldn't like to see him get into any trouble that he couldn't get out of."

"What kind of trouble?" I asked.

He looked uncomfortable, as though he didn't quite trust me, a stranger, and a non-Texan, at that. But after a moment he went on. "Jay McCain's in town." He squinted hard, hoping to learn whether or not I was in on the story.

"Where is he?"

"One of the saloons, most likely. Didn't see him myself."

I looked at the old man closely. He seemed genuinely concerned about what McCain might do to the kid if they came together. After a moment I clapped him lightly on the shoulder and tried to grin. "Let's not worry about it tonight. I was thinking of going into town anyway to kind of look the place over."

He seemed relieved as I walked off. There was no explaining why an old man like Sandy would go out of his way to protect a kid like Phil Carney. But the fact that he had bothered gave me a better insight into the Carney family. Here in Sabina they were more than just a family. They were royalty—fallen royalty, maybe, but royalty just the same. The commoners, like old Sandy, were privileged to serve the name, in much the same way that British subjects served the crown, with unquestioning loyalty. It seemed incredible to me, but that's how things were, and I realized now that I had been aware of it from the moment I had stepped out of the stage that afternoon. It was in the air about the kid, wherever he moved. It was to be seen in sudden grins, hearty handshakes.

They haven't realized yet, I thought wryly, that the King is dead. But Phil Carney couldn't trade on his father's name forever. Once they realized that and turned on him . . . it wouldn't be nice.

It occurred to me then, for the first time, that maybe Phil had already thought of this, and Laura, too. Maybe he could see that his days on the throne were numbered and that the House of

Carney would surely fall if he could not some-how win back his lost kingdom.

I had never thought of it that way. It explained a lot of things that I hadn't understood before. Maybe the kid was growing up. Maybe he was at last accepting the responsibility that he had shunned before.

And maybe the sun will rise in the west tomorrow! I thought.

Why was I kidding myself? He was a wild, spoiled, irresponsible kid, and that's all he would ever be, probably. If I had any sense I'd forget him. And that sister of his. And I'd park on the steps of the stage office and wait for the coach to come in, and then I'd leave Sabina for good. If I had any sense.

What I did was keep walking up the rutted street, toward the main part of town.

There were only two saloons in Sabina. One of them was called the Silver Spur, a shabby shack near the wagon yard, where teamsters gathered and cow hands could get that one last drink before heading back for another six-week stretch in some line camp. The other place just had a plank sign over the door that said, "Bar," and when I heard the click of poker chips I knew I had the right place. It was pretty much like any other saloon except that there was a woman behind the front bar, which was something of a surprise. In the back of the place there were two cow hands

55

punching balls around on a pool table; a chuck-a-luck table, vacant; and two poker tables, only one getting any attention. Six men sat studying their cards, and a red-haired girl sat back a way, watching the game. There was no one at all at the bar until I stepped up and asked for whisky.

The woman behind the bar brought out the bottle and tumbler and let me pour for myself. "You're the one that came in with the Carney boy today?" she said.

"That's right."

"You fought in Virginia, then. That's where Carney was, they say."

"Yes, Virginia mostly."

I was watching the poker game and not paying much attention to the bar girl. Four of the six players I pegged right away as local ranchers or businessmen. One of the others was a very tall, frail-looking man who sat like a dress-shop dummy with his hat pulled down over his eyes. The other was also tall but in no way frail. He was built on bullish lines; thick, heavy shoulders and no waist at all to speak of. All of them were dressed pretty much alike, narrow-brimmed hats and worn trousers and boots and collarless shirts. They didn't go in for black broadcloth and ruffled linen in Sabina. If I'd had to guess, I would have picked the tall, frail man as Jay McCain. All of them wore revolvers in open holsters, as casually as a riverman would wear his shirt.

I didn't know what day of the week it was, but it was a slack one for Sabina saloons. One of the players got up and left the game, and no other customers came in. The two ranch hands were still punching balls around on the pool table. I went back and took a chair next to the red-haired girl who was watching the game, and the bull-shouldered man glanced at me and said:

"There's an open seat, if you want to sit in."

"No, thanks, not tonight."

He shrugged, looked at his cards, and threw them in. There was very little money in the game and they were just playing to kill time, but I was still too broke to sit in. I watched them play out two hands and learned nothing. You can't tell about a gambler in a game like that. After a while I felt the red-haired girl watching me.

She said, "Are you good for a drink, mister?"

She had a very small nose and a large mouth and plenty of freckles that not even several layers of rice powder could hide. She was just another saloon girl and I started to turn her down, and then I decided that I might as well talk to her; maybe I could learn something about the gambler. "All right," I said, "but don't choose anything expensive."

"Do you want to watch the game?"

"Not particularly."

We took a table over by the wall and the bar girl was there to meet us with whisky for me and a glass of pinkish wine for the girl. The red-haired girl took a sip of her wine, looking at me over the edge of her glass. "You must be Cap'n Denfield," she said. "I heard some such man got off the stage with young Carney today." She grinned. "I'm Kate Masters."

She wasn't bad-looking when she grinned, and would have been almost pretty if it hadn't been for that scaly rice powder. Her dress was an overly fancy décolleté affair with yellow tassels on the shoulders and waist and with a dowdy but enormous satin bow on one hip. The doxie's uniform from San Francisco to the Battery. She couldn't have been more than twenty-two or twenty-three. Still watching me, she said, "Why did you come to Sabina, Cap'n?"

There are a lot of things I could have said and intended to say, but what came out was "I'm not sure. I wish I knew myself."

She sat back and laughed. "I know what you mean. I came here two years ago and I've been wondering why ever since."

"Have you been working here for two years?"

"Just about." She liked to talk, and I was in the mood to listen—until it got to be too much. I was glad enough to forget the past three years, and the Carneys, and all the rest of it, and just sit back and let her talk flow around me. During the next several minutes Kate Masters told me that she had been born up north on the Brazos and her family had moved down to the brush country after the Mexican war. Her father and brother had died for the Confederacy, and her mother had died of the milk fever a year later. Their haywire ranch had gone downhill during the war. The herd drifted and the cattle became wild again and couldn't be found. That was about the time that Kate gave up ranching and came to Sabina to go to work in the saloon.

With someone else telling it, the story would have been maudlin and depressing, but Kate Masters had a sense of humor. She knew that I didn't believe a word of the story, but it didn't worry her at all.

I said, half seriously, because she was young and there was still an aura of freshness about her, "Couldn't you find something better than this saloon?" I remembered that Laura Carney had been placed in about the same position, but she had found a place for herself in a boardinghouse.

She shrugged, looking into her glass.

For just a moment I wondered what the real story was about Kate Masters, and then decided that it didn't matter. After a while she finished her wine and went back to where she had been sitting at first, and that was when I noticed that she had eyes for no one but the bull-shouldered man at the poker table.

After it was all over I realized that I had spent my money for wine and whisky and all I had learned was that a fancy girl—who claimed that she wasn't one—was in love with a gambler. My interest in the matter was almost nonexistent. And pretty soon my interest in the Carney mix-up began to shrivel, and I began thinking again of that stage that would be pulling out of Sabina in a matter of hours.

I half expected Phil Carney to track me down and see how I was doing, but almost an hour went by and he didn't show up. I watched the gamblers for a while, but there was nothing to be learned from a game like that, so finally I forced myself to think about the fix the kid had got himself into. I could now understand why he wanted that ranch so desperately. It was the largest and most profitable ranch in this part of Texas, and that was reason enough for me. The thing that made me wonder was this marriage contract of Laura Carney's. Would a woman actually trade herself to a man she must hate just to put her kid brother back in the ranching business?

Apparently she would. But it was difficult to believe. I was trying to figure it out when the trouble started at the poker table.

I don't know how it started; I wasn't even watching the game at the time. Then I heard the red-haired girl saying, "You can't talk to me like that! I won't stand for it!"

For a moment it looked as if that would be the end of it. She had been talking, I guessed, to the bull-shouldered man, but the gambler didn't even seem to know she was there. The girl was standing now, about half a stride from where the gambler was sitting. I could see anger flashing in those blue eyes of hers. The gambler, without even looking around, drew two cards to his hand, and then when the betting started he sort of shrugged and tossed his cards in with the deadwood. Finally he turned in his chair, not even looking at the girl. "Just stay away from me," he said. "When I happen to want a doxie, I'll call for one."

She would have slapped him, but she never got the chance. The gambler half lifted himself off the chair. He shifted his weight quickly, swinging his arm as though he were batting a fly, and the girl went flying back toward the pool table. It happened too fast for anybody to stop it, even if anybody had been in the mood to try. The bull-shouldered gambler, I gathered, had proved himself nobody to fool with.

The girl hit the pool table and bounced like rubber. She came flying back at the gambler and I could see anger catch fire in his eyes. He wasn't playing this time. He swung with the full power of those massive shoulders and struck the girl in the face with the back of his hand. "Goddamn you!" The words seemed to rip themselves from his throat. The girl was on her knees now. In sudden rage, the gambler waded in to hit her again.

It seemed that nobody was going to stop him, until a voice said sharply, "That's enough!"

It was a voice that seemed wound up with anger of its own. The words were flat and surprisingly loud, like the sudden crack of a bull whip, and it sounded as if it meant business. I saw the woman behind the bar looking at me. Then the men at the poker table and the pool table looked at me, and the gambler's blow stopped in mid-air. Then, very deliberately, the gambler turned around and looked at me too.

"What did you say?" he asked hoarsely.

"I said that's enough." I recognized the voice now. It was mine.

"Do you aim to deal yourself in, mister?" the gambler asked softly.

"That will depend on you."

It meant nothing to me. A fancy girl, a gambler. Girls like that get knocked around plenty; it's one of the hazards of their occupation. It didn't mean a single thing to me—and I was in it up to my neck. That's what comes of living too long in the deep South. All women are ladies in the river country, and all men are gentlemen. That's the way the story goes, anyway. You're born to it and it's drilled into you. Protect the lady's honor and don't bother to look at the paint and rice powder on her face. A gentleman doesn't stop to wonder what the consequences will be; he stands up and says, "Sir!"

My trouble was that I wasn't in the river country now, but I had forgotten that for a moment, and that slip of memory had put me in the middle of a private battle. The thing that surprised me, though, was that I was not entirely sorry that it had happened. I had liked the red-haired girl. I liked her grin and her freckles and her sense of humor, and I didn't like seeing her knocked to the floor by a bull-shouldered gambler. So there was more to it than just reflex. The anger in my voice was genuine.

Maybe six seconds had passed since the gambler had landed his last blow, and I knew that I had plunged in all the way. If the water was hot, I had nobody to blame but myself. For one tense moment it looked as if the only thing for us to do was go for our revolvers. Bet everything we had on the single turn of a card. Probably that's what we would have done if we hadn't both been gamblers. A gambler wants to know his man, he wants to know the odds. And there we were, two strangers, one of us a flick of the wrist from death.

The pot was too big. He wasn't going to bet his stack until he had a look at the hole card.

I don't know how long that moment lasted; it seemed like a long time. In the back of my mind I was aware of the other players backing away, getting out of the line of fire, and the two pool players were backing away, too. The red-haired girl was the only one who didn't move. She knelt on the floor, holding herself up with one hand. Her lips were puffy and a small trickle of crimson had formed at the corner of her mouth and was dripping slowly down her chin. The woman behind the bar had disappeared. She had ducked down among the bottles somewhere, out of sight. I also noticed that the tall, frail-looking man was grinning faintly, vaguely amused at the proceedings. He looked at me and shook his head slowly from side to side, as though he were already seeing me laid out in a pine box.

The frail man was surprised at the way it ended. He didn't quite believe it when the bull-shouldered man finally began to relax, when he saw that he wasn't going to grab for his revolver and that there was going to be no blood spilled after all. The frail man was disappointed. He'd had great confidence in his big friend, he had been sure that he could take me. The others had been thinking the same thing. Their mouths came open when they saw that the big gambler wasn't going to draw.

"That was a mistake, mister," he said in a voice that shook with rage.

There was nothing I could say to that. It was entirely possible that he was right.

He said, "I don't like people stickin' their noses into my business."

"And I don't like to see ladies kicked around."

He made a noise that might have been laughter,

but there was no humor in his eyes. The moment was over now. He was angry that he had let it get away from him. He was afraid that the others would think that he had backed down from a fight. Still, I could see that the moment was over. Maybe tomorrow would be another day and he would get to thinking about it and come after me. But not now. There's no betting a hand once it's thrown in.

He said, "You want some advice, mister?" And he took three slow steps in my direction. But all the menace was in his eyes and not in his cupped hand near the butt of his .44. "Listen," he said. "There's a coach leavin' Sabina tomorrow mornin'. I think you ought to be on it."

He had nothing showing, but there was still his hole card and he was trying to run me out on that. He was still betting that he could regain some of his lost dignity. All he had to do was prove to the others that he could make me back down or run me out of town. But there is a gambler's rule that says never let a man take the first pot on a bluff.

I said, "I'm afraid my visit won't be over by tomorrow."

I'd raised, and now he had to call or throw in. It was a tough hand to play. He had noticed the remnants of my Confederate uniform and he must have known that I had at least a speaking acquaintance with firearms. How good I was he'd never know unless he plunged with me—and I knew by now that he was no plunger unless he could get all the odds on his side.

I heard the breath whistling through his teeth. "Have it any way you want it," he said hoarsely. "Don't say I didn't warn you."

That was the end of it. He didn't like it, but there was not much he could do since he had made up his mind to play it close to the vest. With a jerk of his head, he motioned for the frail man to follow him, and the two of them walked the length of the saloon and through the door.

I took three quick, deep breaths of air. I felt as if I had been several minutes underwater.

"Well!" somebody said, and then there was a nervous titter and the place began to come to life. The poker game had broken up. The players were raking in their chips, both relieved and disappointed that there had been no fight. The woman came up from behind the bar, holding a sawed-off shotgun in both hands. When she saw that she wouldn't need it, she put it down and wiped her face with a bar towel.

"Mister," she said huskily, "I guess you don't realize just how much trouble you almost got into." She came around the end of the bar, shaking her head. "Why did you do it?"

"Miss," I said seriously, "I wish I knew."

We stood there looking at each other. She was fat, but it was hard, firm fat, and she was almost as tall as I was. She shook her head again. "Do you know who that man was?"

"Jay McCain?" I asked.

"Do you mean you acted the way you did, knowing who he was?" From the way she said it, I got a pretty good idea what kind of reputation McCain had.

We had almost forgotten the girl who had started it all. Finally I remembered her and went to the back of the place, where she was still kneeling, staring blankly at the floor. The fat woman came back with the towel and I wiped the blood off the red-haired girl's face and helped her to her feet. She looked at me and I could see her eyes going in and out of focus.

"Are you all right?" I asked.

"You shouldn't have tried to help me," she said. "Jay will kill you. I know how he is. He'll think about it and think about it, and then he'll come after you."

"You'd better let me worry about that," I said. "Where do you live? I'll see that you get home."

"She lives with me," the fat woman said. "I have a little place on the cross street behind the saloon, but I can't leave the bar now."

"I'll attend to it." I took the girl's arm and the fat woman took us to the back door and showed us how to get to her place. It was just a little clapboard shack sitting behind the line of business buildings. I held onto the girl's arm and she followed along, unprotesting, as we stumbled over the rubble that you always find in back alleys. When we reached the shack I opened the door and then went inside and found a lamp and lit it. There were only two rooms in the place. The walls were papered with newspapers to help keep out the wind and dust, and there was an iron bed and a small cookstove and not much else. The girl had followed me in and now she sat on the bed, still staring at me with those wide, hurt eyes.

"Will you be all right now?" I asked.

She nodded her head. Then she lay across the bed and suddenly she began to laugh, but it was not like any laughter that I had ever heard before. After a moment the sound stopped. "Thanks," she said.

For what, I didn't ask. "I guess I knew it would end like this," she said flatly. "But this is the first time he ever hit me. The very first time." As though it were something to be proud of.

I felt uncomfortable and slightly sick. I mumbled something, and turned toward the door to go. The side of her face was turning blue, and her mouth would not be a pretty thing the next morning. Oh, McCain was quite a man, all right. At that moment I was sorry that he hadn't made that fatal move for his gun. Maybe he could have beaten me, but I felt willing to take the chance.

"He used to love me," she said, in that same flat voice. "He used to tell me I was pretty. I wasn't, of course, but it was nice to hear, and he can be nice when he wants to. We were going to be married; he told me we'd be married and he would take me back to the place he came from, Kansas, I think. And he would have done it, maybe, if it hadn't been for her."

She wasn't talking to me. She was just talking, and I stood there listening because I didn't know what else to do.

"Laura Carney," she said. "What would a woman like that want with a man like McCain?"

I could have told her, but what was the use? And probably she wouldn't have understood it any better than I did. I stood there for a moment and she didn't make another sound or look at me, and after a while I opened the door and went out. Well, I thought, this is a fine mess. But I had nobody to blame but myself. I'd have to remember that when McCain finally decided to take the plunge and come gunning for me.

The night was surprisingly cool. I stood in front of the girl's shack, looking up at the darkness and listening to the small sounds that always come with the night. Looking back at the saloon incident, I thought it was still a damn-fool stunt, just the kind of thing some hotheaded juvenile would have tried—but I still wasn't sorry. I guess I just didn't like McCain.

I began walking back toward Sabina's business district. There was a gap between the saloon and a feed store on the other side, and I started between the buildings thinking it would be a short cut to the Charleston House. There was only about three feet of clearance between the buildings, as dark as an ink well, and when I was about halfway through I discovered that I was not alone. Somebody had come in behind me. I stopped and turned, my hand brushing the butt of that old Griswold and Grier. And then somebody came in from the other end. I didn't hear him until it was too late. I was about to draw the revolver and find out who it was that I was facing when the sky fell.

Later, thinking back on it, I imagined that I had heard the smallest whisper of a sound, the gentle swish of a pistol slicing through the still, black air. It was only in imagination, probably. Anyway, it was too late. The pistol barrel crashed down on the crown of my old Confederate campaign hat, and then against my skull, and that was the last I remembered.

Chapter Four

I was just as glad that the first blow had put me out and I hadn't been conscious through the rest of it. Whoever had been wielding the pistol hadn't stopped with one swing. My cheek was split, there was a cut on the back of my head, and my mouth would never be quite the same again.

When I opened my eyes there was a gentle breeze moaning through the narrow passageway. My friends had left me. I lay there for a long while, listening to the thunder inside my head, not trying to figure it out, just marveling that I was still alive. It's the easiest thing in the world to pistol-whip a man to death. A man's skull is softer than gun steel. It's as simple as that.

I sat up and was suddenly sick. Several minutes went by before I began piecing things together. The first name I thought of was Jay McCain, and that seemed to be the beginning and the end to the problem. I had somehow managed to live through battles like Yellow Tavern and The Wilderness and Bloody Angle, only to come to a place called Sabina and almost get killed in an alley beside a saloon. Slowly—very slowly—I lifted myself and leaned against the feed store and concentrated on dragging cool air into my lungs. I reached for my neckerchief to wipe the blood off my face, but I wasn't wearing a neckerchief. I began going through my pockets, looking for something, and that was when I found the piece of paper. It was too dark to see what kind of paper it was. I only knew that it hadn't been in my pocket before the beating. After a while I made my way out to the plank walk, to the orange lantern light coming through the saloon window, and I looked at the paper again. It was a ticket for the morning stage.

Strangely, up until that time I hadn't felt any

anger or any other kind of emotion. Now it began to come. It came up from my groin as bitter as gall and I could taste it in my throat. Anger. It pulled taut the muscles along my neck and shoulders and chest, constricting my breathing and bringing the nerve ends to the top of my skin. I had never known that kind of anger before. I had never been pistol-whipped before. I had never been invited to get out of a town before. I had to come to Sabina for that!

I thought: All right, McCain, we'll settle it right now, once and for all! And by God, we won't settle it with beatings and stage tickets, we'll settle it with business ends of revolvers! I will not be bullied out of Sabina or anywhere else! I will stay planted on this cursed edge of nowhere until I rot, if I feel like it, I'll be goddamned if I won't!

And even as I thought it I knew that I was in no condition to fight anybody, much less a man like McCain. I could barely stand. My head was splitting and something had happened to my eyes; objects kept advancing and receding, and everything was blurred. My common sense told me to stay right where I was until I got to feeling better. Until I could walk. Then it told me to go back to the Charleston House and see how badly I was hurt. Tomorrow would be another day. Tomorrow Mr. McCain would still be in Sabina, and so would I, but one of us wasn't going to be here long.

I started walking. I passed people on the street and they stood back with their mouths open. Welcome to Sabina, I thought. That kid, that goddamn Phil Carney, he's the one I ought to kill. If it weren't for him I'd be in the river country right this minute, watching the side-wheelers plow ponderously through the muddy water, listening to the throaty singing of the darkies, sitting at a felt-topped table with the kind of men I know. And then I thought: Oh, no, you wouldn't, Denfield. You came here of your own accord. Remember?

The thoughts slipped in and out of my mind like wind going through a canyon. I kept walking. I passed a general store, then I stopped and went back and looked through the plate-glass window. The store was also the stage office. In the back of the place I could see a little whiskered man bending over a roll-top desk, doing some paper work in the light of a single flickering lamp. I knocked on the glass. When the storekeeper didn't look up, I took out my revolver and rapped the glass a few times with the barrel.

That got him up. He came forward, stooped and squinting, and then he opened the door and his eyes went wide. "Christamighty!" he said. "What happened to you, mister?"

"I want to know if anybody bought a stage ticket here. It couldn't have been more than an hour ago."

"A shoe drummer came in a while back and got a ticket to Minco, the next place on the line."

I took the paper from my pocket and handed it to him. "This is the ticket I mean. Who bought it?"

He looked at it and his eyes began to get that careful look. "I reckon I don't know about that one."

"You've got a short memory. It was bought less than an hour ago."

"Look," he said nervously, "the stage office has been closed since six o'clock. I got work to be doin'." He started to close the door, but I put one foot in and held it open. He stood there for a minute, just looking at me. Then he glanced quickly up and down the street. "Slim Kasper," he said quickly. "Now let me lock the door."

"Would Slim Kasper be a very tall, fragile-looking man? A gambling friend of Jay McCain?"

"He might be." I took my foot out of the door. The storekeeper slammed it and then opened it again, all in one motion. "But don't tell him I told you. Is Slim the one that gave you that face?"

By that time I was heading again toward the Charleston House.

Phil Carney was still on the bed, his boots propped on the iron bedstead, when I came in. He dropped his boots to the floor when he saw me.

"Good Lord! What happened to you?"

"Get me some water and a towel. And some soothing salve, if you can find it."

For a moment he just stared. Then he was off the bed like a shot and I could hear his boot heels whacking the stairs as he headed for the kitchen, where the water was kept. He came back with a bucket and dipper and ladled some of the clear water into a crock bowl. "What happened to you? Did you have a fight?"

"You could hardly call it a fight."

Then I told him what had happened, and he sat there on the bed with his mouth open while I sponged the blood and dirt from my face. I put some salve on my split cheek, then I tore a little piece off the towel to put over it, and finally I covered the whole thing with a piece of sticking plaster. The place on my head didn't seem bad enough for all that trouble. There was a good-sized lump and a piece of the scalp was broken, but the healing salve, I figured, would do for the time being. There was nothing much I could do about the split lips and the bruises.

The kid stood up when I finished the story. "Joseph and Mary!" he said. "Why did you have to take the part of a saloon girl?"

"Why does a man do anything? Why did I come to Sabina?"

"And you think it was McCain?"

"I'm sure of it; his friend bought the ticket. It

looks like he wanted to try one more bluff before betting the stack."

"What are you goin' to do now?"

I looked up, holding the towel to my mouth. "Kill a gambler."

Phil Carney laughed. I didn't see anything funny, but he threw his head back and roared. "That's exactly what I said once," he said when he got his breath, "and you thought I was crazy!"

"That was different. You would have been no match for a man like McCain. Maybe I will be."

"And maybe you won't," he said, soberly now. The whole thing had got turned around somehow. Now I was the wild-eyed one and the kid was the one trying to keep things in check. "Think about the ranch," he said.

I didn't give a tinker's damn about the ranch, and he could see it. "All right," he said evenly. "Think about Laura." He stood there looking at me, playing it for all it was worth. He would have made a wonderful gambler if he had been older and more settled, because he knew instinctively what kind of things go on in a man's mind. He knew, for instance, that sometimes a dream can be more real and more persistent than reality itself.

I said, "I'm going to get some sleep."

He didn't argue. All he wanted was the ranch, and he didn't want McCain for a brother-in-law, and he knew that it would do no good to argue. Plant the seed of old desire and let it grow. That was the best way. I wondered if Phil Carney had any idea how deep that instinctive wisdom of his really went.

I lay awake for a long time after the lamp had been pinched out, feeling my well of strength, my anger, slowly running dry. If I had wanted to kill McCain, I should have done it as soon as I was able to walk out of the alley. Tomorrow, I knew now, I wouldn't have the stomach for it. I would hesitate, I would wait for McCain to come after me, putting myself on the defensive. A great many cemeteries were filled with men who had decided at the last minute to go on the defensive.

There is still the morning stage, I thought.

But I was holding firm to that part of it. I would be damned if I would let anybody run me out of town, like a hound with its tail between its legs. And I wouldn't soon forget that pistol whipping, either. You might as well stop thinking about it, I thought. To get satisfaction from McCain, you'll have to either kill him or break him. And the only way to break him is through gambling. . . .

The room was dark and Phil Carney was only a humped-up ridge on the other bed. I couldn't see his face, but I could feel him grinning. You'll get your goddamn ranch, I thought. I'll take it from McCain if I have to use every underhanded trick known to gambling. When I get through with him he'll wish he'd never heard of Sabina—but don't think I'm doing it because of you. And don't think you're so smart, either. Your sister has nothing to do with this. No matter what you may think.

He was still grinning, I could feel it. Who are you kidding, Denfield?

The first thing I saw when I opened my eyes the next morning was Phil Carney standing at the foot of the bed. He was holding a leather bag—not a very big one—slapping it slowly, monotonously into the palm of his hand. When he saw that I was awake, he tossed the bag at me.

"That's what you'll have to start with," he said.

I loosened the drawstring and saw that the pouch was full of gold coins; double eagles, they looked like, and I guessed that there must be about two thousand dollars there. It had been a long time since I had held that much money.

I put the money aside and swung to a sitting position. I felt like hell—just the way I had known I would feel. Every move I made touched off a chain reaction in my ragged nerves. It even hurt to blink my eyes. Finally I got up and looked in the dresser mirror, and I didn't look any better than I felt. The bruises that had been only slightly discolored the night before were now a patchwork of ugly greens and browns. The left side of my face was swollen and the eye was almost closed.

I said, "Have you heard anything?"

"The story's already made the rounds. There was talk at breakfast that McCain had invited you to leave town."

"What else?"

He shrugged. "That's about all. The citizens will be expectin' a shoot-out, most likely, if you're not on that mornin' stage." He grinned very faintly. "The stage has already pulled out," he added.

It looked like Phil Carney had finally got on his own track and was running true to form. He hadn't taken any chances on my backing out at the last minute; he had simply let me sleep past stagetime. Well, I thought, the lines are drawn now. If McCain has made his brags, he can't pull out of this thing any easier than I can. I began pulling on my clothes. There was a knock on the door, and the kid jumped, almost as though he had been expecting it. Then the door opened and it was Laura Carney.

She hadn't lost her knack of looking right through me and not seeing me. She looked at her brother and said, "There's no time to lose. Sandy Potts has his hack out back. He has agreed to make the trip to Minco."

I didn't know what she was talking about, but the kid did. "Laura thinks you're no match for McCain," he said, with that half grin of his. "She figures you'd better go to Minco and wait for the next stage there."

I said, "Maybe it's time I started making up my own mind about what I should do or shouldn't do."

She saw me then. She turned quickly and fixed those clear, dark eyes on me. I wondered if I would ever see her any way but angry. "Mr. Denfield," she said—almost hissed—"I am doing what I think best. You can do nothing in Sabina but cause trouble."

"Am I supposed to laugh off this beating I took last night?"

"It's better than getting killed, isn't it?" she asked coldly. "Now please hurry. Sandy is waiting for you at the back door."

"Tell Sandy to go home," I said. "I won't be leaving Sabina today."

She froze at that. She was a girl used to getting her way, but she wasn't getting it today. McCain wasn't running me out of town, and that was that. I swung my revolver around my waist and buckled it, and then I picked up the leather pouch and stuffed it into my waistband. I expected her to try to stop me when I walked out of the room, but she didn't. I don't know how much the kid had told her or if he had told her anything. She just stood there watching me and I went into the hallway and down the stairs.

Breakfast was over and the parlor was empty. Well, I wasn't hungry anyway. I went outside on the front porch and a cow hand sat half asleep in one of the rockers, a whittled toothpick drooping from the corner of his mouth. He looked at me and his eyes became interested. When I started up the street, he lifted himself out of the chair and followed.

Was he another one of McCain's friends? I doubted it. He had probably heard the story about last night and was just curious to see what would happen next. I met a few people on the sidewalk and they all backed away and gave me plenty of room. A few minutes later I looked back and all of them were following. They weren't passing up the chance to see a gun fight, in case one developed.

I had almost reached the saloon when Kate Masters, red-haired fancy girl, came out of a doorway and stepped in front of me.

"Are you crazy?" she demanded. "Do you *want* to be killed?"

Her left cheek was swollen and discolored, but it didn't look as bad as mine. She took hold of my arm. "Listen to me," she said. "I appreciate what you tried to do last night, but that's all over now." She looked at my face and shook her head. "Don't you know by now that Jay means business? He'll kill you."

I took her arm as gently as I could and moved her out of the way and went on into the saloon. There was quite a crowd waiting outside, so I knew that McCain must be on the inside, waiting for me.

The tall, sleepy-looking man was at the bar when I came in. I put the stage ticket on the boards in front of him. "You'd better get your money back on this. I won't be using it."

He merely smiled. It wasn't his argument.

Slim Kasper was the only customer at the bar and the only other man in the house besides McCain. The gambler was sitting at one of the round poker tables in the back of the place, idly sifting a stack of chips through his left hand. His right hand was in his lap. He sat far enough back from the table so that it wouldn't be in his way, and his revolver was pulled around in front for what the badmen call a "saddle" or "cross-arm" draw. He was completely confident. The woman behind the bar stared at one of us and then the other, trying to decide whether she should step in and try to stop it. Then she began backing toward the front of the bar and I knew that she had decided that it was none of her business.

I glanced at her and said, "Bourbon," and threw the leather pouch on the bar. "Have you got a safe here that I could keep my money in? It's more than I'd like to be carrying around."

She lifted the pouch and made a small whistling sound, almost forgetting the trouble that was crowding her. "That's a lot of money, mister."

"Almost two thousand. Gold."

She poured the drink and I picked it up with my left hand. Watching McCain, I talked to the woman. "I kind of like it here in Sabina. My mind's set on buying a ranch down here and maybe settling down."

She knew that I wasn't talking for her benefit, but she played along. With that much gold around, she was betting that some of it would get sidetracked into the saloon. She picked up the pouch, weighing it again in the palm of her hand. "That's a lot of money," she said again, "but not hardly enough for a good ranch. If that's what you had in mind."

"I figured to run it up to enough. If there's anybody in Sabina willing to gamble for my kind of money."

The bait was out and the trap was set, but I couldn't help wondering just who was the hunter and who was the hunted. Slim Kasper laughed softly. He probably knew that it would be very difficult for a man like McCain to deliberately turn down two thousand in gold. The situation amused him.

I paid no attention to Kasper. Sooner or later, I thought, I'll settle the pistol whipping, but McCain was the one I was interested in now. He hadn't moved since I'd entered the saloon, except to sift those chips back and forth through his left hand. He had expected quick action. An accusation, a burst of anger, and sudden shooting. But it hadn't worked that way. He now had a choice, where he hadn't expected one. What did he want most—the satisfaction of killing me, or the two thousand in gold?

It took a little while for him to make up his mind. Oh, he hated me, all right, because I had backed him down in front of the town and had injured his reputation as a hardcase. On the other hand, he would like to have that money. There were a lot of things a man could do with that much gold.

At that moment I heard boot heels hit the plank walk. Then the batwings swung open and a hoarse, tough voice said, "What's goin' on here?"

I didn't look around and neither did McCain, but Slim Kasper said gently, "Why, nothin', Marshal. It seems like we're just about to sit down to a little poker game. You care to sit in?" The heavy tramp of boots came closer and a big hand grasped my shoulder and jerked me around.

"I asked a question," he said angrily. "What's goin' on here?"

He was a big man, bigger than Jay McCain, and heavier, and much tougher. There was a town marshal's star pinned to his leather vest, and an enormous Tucker, Sherrod .44-caliber Dragoon with a silver star set into the wooden grip hung at his side. The red-haired saloon girl had come in beside him.

There was a touchy moment of silence. For a brief instant I saw anger flare up behind McCain's eyes. Kate Masters, by bringing in the Marshal, had taken away his choice. I didn't know who the Marshal was, but I knew that there would be no shoot-out as long as he was there. The flash of anger burned away and I could almost see what the gambler was thinking. If I was fool enough to

84

gamble with him, why shouldn't he take my money? There would always be tomorrow. Plenty of time for settling grudges. And McCain was one who wouldn't likely forget a grudge. He sat back in his chair, tasting the compromise and finding it to his liking. Take my money and *then* kill me! That was the smart way to handle it!

He even smiled, very faintly. "That's right, Marshal. We was just talkin' about startin' a little game."

The Marshal didn't like it, but he didn't know just what to do. He turned from me to McCain, his voice rough and his face hard. "Look here, McCain, just don't try to start anything. I've been out all night chasin' cow thieves across the river. I haven't had any sleep and my temper's touchy."

"I told you it's just a game, Marshal. Ask the stranger there."

"Just remember what I said." He glared at me and then at the red-haired girl who had brought him in. He looked sour on the world and aching for a fight. McCain wasn't ready to oblige him and neither was I, and finally he turned on his heel and tramped out of the saloon. Slim Kasper laughed again, softly, but not until the Marshal was well out of hearing. He smiled thinly at the woman behind the bar.

"Break a new deck for us, Stella. We might as well get the game started, like we told the Marshal." The red-haired Kate Masters stood rigidly, staring at McCain. It isn't often that you see as much hate as she put in that one look.

Slim Kasper walked over to the table and sat down opposite McCain, and Stella got a new deck from under the bar and broke the seal.

"Are you still lookin' for somebody to gamble for your kind of money, Denfield?" McCain asked gently.

"The three of us?"

He shrugged. "There'll be more after a while."

"Just the two of us, McCain; me and you." I looked around and saw Kate Masters still standing beside the bar. "And the girl will keep the bank."

He didn't like that. He had counted on doubling the odds against me by having Kasper playing on the other side. But he was still confident, and his anger was in check. With another shrug, he said, "Whatever you say," and Kasper pushed his chair back a few inches to signify that he was to be dealt around. "A hundred to start with?" McCain asked, and I nodded.

The saloon girl sat on my side of the table, keeping the bank in a tin cigar can. Without looking at McCain, she took our gold and counted out our chips. I didn't suggest a house dealer because I didn't know one that I could trust. McCain glanced up as he riffled the new deck.

"Stud?"

I cut and he began to deal.

The curious were beginning to come into the

saloon, now that it looked like there would be no shooting. They showed surprise when they saw me and McCain squared off across the poker table. But not Phil Carney, when he came in. The kid moved in quietly and stood by the table with the others, grinning that faint half grin of his. Carney had almost enough faith in my gambling ability to do for both of us. He had gone to a lot of trouble to get me to Sabina, and he was clearly confident that I could somehow get his ranch back and everything would be settled.

Within an hour I had lost my first hundred and was having to buy more chips from Kate Masters. By that time we had collected quite a crowd. It was more than just a poker game, and they knew it, because they knew Jay McCain. Most of them, I guessed, hated McCain's guts, but strangely enough, they seemed to be on his side. A thing like that is pretty hard to explain, and about the only way you can explain it is to say that they just didn't care much for strangers in Sabina. Too, their estimate of me had gone down when I had failed to come into the saloon shooting, as they had expected. I had let them down, and on top of that I was a river man.

McCain represented Sabina for most of them. That they hated his guts didn't seem to matter. Through some kind of primitive logic they had broken the thing down to its simplest form and were making it a contest of Texas poker against river poker. There was a muted grunting of approval when I had to go back to the bank for more chips. I had two people on my side—Phil Carney and the red-haired Kate Masters—and neither of them made a sound.

It was my deal and I dealt the down cards and the up cards and took a look at the hole. I found myself thinking about that saloon girl. It isn't often that you see a woman change the way she had changed. Yesterday she had looked at Jay McCain with the liquid, calflike eyes of those who are very naïve and very much in love. Today there was only a flatness in those eyes, a look of shock. While I thought of that, I lost another hand.

Wake up, Denfield. With this kind of playing, the kid's two-thousand-dollar stake isn't going to last long!

But Phil Carney wasn't worried. This was my poker strategy, he thought. Let McCain win for a while, build up false confidence, and then draw him into a big pot where it counted. That would have been all right for some men, but not with McCain. He was no haywire nester or reckless cow hand; he was a professional gambler, and a good one, at that.

By the time I was halfway through my second stack of chips, I began to wonder if he wasn't a little too good, if his luck wasn't just a little more than it ought to be. The cards showed no signs of crimping or smudging or marking, and I had watched his hands like a hawk against the possibility of second dealing. When it came my turn to handle the cards I stacked them and looked at the edges.

I glanced at McCain. Then I cut the cards myself, feeling along the edges with my fingers, and the card that I cut was an ace. The edge had been spread, very slightly and expertly, but enough. My anger wasn't at McCain, but at myself for not having noticed it before. I pushed the cards aside and asked for a new deck.

Nobody noticed it but McCain, myself, and possibly Kate Masters. I saw the quick flash of rage behind the gambler's eyes, but he was quick to hide it. The incident had taught each of us something. McCain now knew that I was a professional gambler, for a pastime poker player would never have noticed that spread ace. And I knew that Phil Carney had actually been cheated out of his ranch.

Chapter Five

It was long after dark when the game broke up. Phil Carney and I stood on the plank walk outside the saloon watching the scattered lights of Sabina go out one by one. My back ached, my shoulders were stiff, and my brain was muddy from poring over the cards since midmorning.

Still, I felt good. I had won back my money and had more than a hundred of McCain's. The kid took a sack of makings and each of us rolled a cigarette. In the flare of a sulphur match, Phil Carney said, "Are you convinced?"

"Of what?"

"That you can take the ranch from McCain."

"I'm not convinced of that at all—a long way from it. But I did learn one thing." And I told him about the incident of the spread ace.

He didn't seem surprised. "I told you I was cheated."

"All right, I believe you now."

We began walking toward the Charleston House. The idlers were coming out of the saloon now that the game was over for the night, and some of them stood watching us, and we could hear them muttering under their breaths. They hated me—actually hated me—because I had taken money from their crooked champion. Oh, Sabina is a fine town! I thought bitterly. I ached in my bones for the lushness of the river country. If I lived to be a hundred I would never get to like this sun-blasted wilderness of brush and gravel that Phil Carney held such store by.

As we neared the Charleston House, I saw Laura Carney standing near the end of the porch. We started to go right into the house, pretending that we hadn't seen her, when she said:

"Mr. Denfield."

I stopped and so did Phil Carney. She said coolly, "I'd like to talk to Mr. Denfield alone, Phil."

Carney thought for a moment, sizing something up in his mind. Then he laughed shortly. "You'd better keep your guard up, Jeff." And he went into the house and up the stairs.

Laura Carney still hadn't moved, so I went down to the end of the porch where she was. It was dark down there. What little moonlight there was was blocked out by a wall of climbing honeysuckle. I said, "You wanted to talk to me, Miss Carney?"

"Are you a gambler?"

"I was before the war."

"But not in this country. Not in Texas."

"No. I rode river boats most of the time."

"Then why did you come to Texas, Mr. Denfield?"

I could almost smile. What would she say, I wondered, if I told her about that creation of perfect womanhood that I had been carrying around in my mind? But I said, "I don't rightly know, Miss Carney."

"Was it Phil's idea? It was, wasn't it? Somehow he persuaded you to come down here and attempt to win the ranch back for him." I must have shown surprise, and then she said, "The story's all over town about how you started gambling with Jay McCain today. Do you know what they're beginning to say, Mr. Denfield?" Her voice was suddenly whiplike, cutting. "They're saying that *I* am the stake you are gambling for! They say that you are trying to *win* me from Jay McCain in a poker game!"

That stunned me for a moment. There was only one way a story like that could get started, and that was through Phil Carney. I thought of that and anger started boiling up. I wasn't prepared for what happened next. I should have learned by now not to be surprised at anything the Carneys might do, but they always managed to stay one stride ahead of me. The next thing I knew there were tears in Laura Carney's eyes. She dropped her head and stood there, all anger gone. Then—I don't know how it happened—I had my arms around her.

She seemed very small. She was shaking, and I held her for what must have been several minutes, and at last the shaking stopped.

A crazy thing had happened.

A dream had come to life, and I was holding her. It was just the way I had imagined it would be. She was just the way I had wanted her to be: beautiful, gentle, needing protection.

I heard myself saying, "It's all right. Everything's going to be all right."

She had her head against my shoulder and I couldn't see her face. "Jeff . . . Do you mind if I call you Jeff?"

"No."

"Jeff, I'm so afraid!"

"There's no need to be afraid."

"I hate him!" And I could feel her shudder.

"McCain?"

"I despise him!"

I wanted to ask why she insisted on marrying him, if she despised him, but she answered my question before I could ask it. "It's because of Phil. Oh, we fight, and never agree on things, but he's my brother. There's always been a streak of wildness in him—you should know that. He would never rest until he got his ranch back. Jay McCain would have killed him. Phil would have forced him to. Don't you see, marrying Jay is the only way I can save my brother!"

I wanted to ask if her brother was worth saving, but I didn't. I held her close, my head swimming with the scent of her hair, my chest pounding at the feel of her against me. The hard shell of her anger had fallen away, and now I could see her as she really was. The way I had imagined her. I said, "You don't have to go through with it if you don't want to."

"But there's no other way!"

"There's gambling."

I hadn't meant to say it because I wasn't at all sure that gambling would do it. But when she clung to me, pressed her softness against me, I felt that there was nothing that I couldn't do.

"Do you . . . do you think you could?"

"I can try. I can try hard." And if gambling wouldn't do it, there was always my revolver. A revolver wouldn't get the ranch back, but it would take care of McCain, and that was what I was interested in. I felt her arms around my neck. Suddenly she kissed me. The kiss was full of sweetness and fire and I held her savagely for a moment, almost crushing her.

And then she was gone. I don't know how. My arms were suddenly empty and I heard the quick sound of her heels as she ran along the porch and into the house.

I stood out there for a long while, hardly moving, breathing in the coolness of the night while I waited for the pounding in my chest to ease. The impossible had happened. By what magic it had been brought about, I didn't know, and I cared less. Denfield, I thought, you must have been blind! The dream had been real all the time, and I hadn't seen it!

For the first time, I was glad that I had come to Sabina. The insanity of the situation seemed to have melted away. It was suddenly clear-cut and logical. There were two things I had to do: First, I had to get back that damned ranch of Phil Carney's, and then I would have to kill Jay McCain. I knew men like McCain and I knew that he would have it no other way. If he lost Laura, he would try to kill me, and it would be up to me to see that he didn't.

As I stood there in the darkness, with the feel of Laura Carney all around me, it all seemed perfectly sensible. And I was supremely confident. I could have whipped the world that night.

I got up for breakfast the next morning. Some of the boarders were roomers who stayed at the Charleston House, but most of them were ranch hands who had spent the night in the livery barn, and a few businessmen who had no wives to cook for them. There was a big round table in the dining room and perhaps a dozen men were beginning to sit down when Phil Carney and I came down from our room. I knew that McCain would be there, so I wasn't surprised when I saw him sitting beside Slim Kasper at the far end of the table.

McCain didn't even look up when we came in, but the others did, and I had a feeling that the room was holding its breath, waiting for something to explode. Nothing happened. Kasper was holding a platter of fried mush, and he smiled sleepily before passing it on, and that's all there was to it. The kid and I found chairs and sat down.

Laura came in with platters of biscuits and fried steak, and I could feel that old ache rising again in my chest. She was really beautiful! How could I have missed that before? She walked like a queen and there was grace in every move she made. She made several trips back and forth from the kitchen, her head bowed, not looking at anyone, and her cheeks were pink with embarrassment. The story was around, all right—I could see it on the faces of the men. Laura Carney was on the block. She was being gambled for like a stack of poker chips. I glanced at Phil Carney and he was calmly cutting into a piece of steak.

It was an uncomfortable meal. Everybody felt the tenseness in the room, and McCain's grimness did nothing to help it. He remained silent throughout the meal, and only the tightness of his mouth betrayed the anger boiling inside him. Sometime during the day our poker game would be picked up where it had been left off last night, but nobody mentioned it. It was taken for granted, and they were all waiting.

Phil Carney handed me the fried potatoes and I passed the platter down the table. "I'll bet," he said under his breath, "this is the quietest breakfast in Texas this mornin'."

I had my eyes on Laura. I couldn't take them off her, and I noticed that McCain couldn't either. She was taking platters off the table now, and the men were beginning to push back their chairs when McCain reached out and took her arm.

"I'm havin' my buggy hitched down at the livery barn," he said loudly. "Tell Mrs. Lorrin' we're goin' for a little ride. We'll be back before dinnertime."

She stood as rigid as stone. Apparently these

buggy rides were the usual procedure, for nobody seemed surprised. Still there was that breathless feeling in the room again as they waited to see whose side Laura was going to be on.

Not looking at him, she said, "I'm afraid I can't go this morning."

I saw crimson crawling up from under the collar of McCain's shirt. "Sure you can," he said tightly. "Just tell Mrs. Lorrin'."

She looked at me for the first time, and behind her eyes there was a silent cry for help. I came half out of my chair, but then she jerked away from McCain and almost ran back to the kitchen.

For several seconds it was absolutely quiet in the dining room. McCain sat in silent rage. He had forced a showdown and had lost. His name as a ladies' man had gone the way of his hardcase reputation. If there had been any point in it, he might have tried his hand at killing me right there in the dining room. Finally Slim Kasper stood up and said, "Let's get over to the saloon, Jay. There might be a game after a while."

The gambler looked at me. "There'd better be!" He pushed his chair back and walked out. The others began filing out then, quietly, as though they were leaving a funeral.

"Don't turn your back to him," Phil Carney said. "He's mad enough to kill you."

The kid followed me out of the room and we stood on the front porch after the others were gone. "You can take McCain," he said calmly. "You took a hundred off him last night without any trouble. Within a week you'll have the ranch back."

That ranch! It was all he could think about.

"I think I'll ride out there today," he said thoughtfully. "It'll be good to see the place again." He glanced at me again, grinning thinly. "You don't even know what I'm talking about, do you, Jeff? You wouldn't understand if I told you a man can starve for land the same as he can starve for food. You don't know what it is to work all day in the sun clearing brush, and then stand back and look at what you've done and know that it's good. You never took over your father's work and kept it goin', did you? I did once. While I was doin' it, it was almost as though my father had never died, as if he was still there, workin' beside me. Maybe that's the only kind of immortality we'll ever know—and if it is, it's good enough for me."

He flipped away a match and dragged deeply on his cigarette. "I know what you think about me, Jeff, and some of it's pretty bad. I've tricked you and lied to you, but I'm not sorry for any of that. I hope you find something you want here in Sabina, but if you don't, it won't make much difference. All I want is that ranch. I don't give a damn about anything else." He burned almost half the cigarette in one furious drag. "I'll be sorry if McCain kills you, but I'll get over it, and after a while, I'll figure out another way to beat him. You said once that you wanted the truth. Well, that's the truth, Jeff."

He shook his head, as though he were amazed at himself. "I just figured it was time you knew. I know how you feel about Laura. I wish I could tell you whether she's in love with you or whether she's just using you, like I am, but I can't. She's my sister, but I never pretended to understand her. That, I guess, will be up to you."

He flipped his cigarette into the yard and walked off toward town. It was crazy, maybe, but at that moment I liked Phil Carney more than I ever had before. I had absolutely no understanding of the way he felt about the ranch. But Laura did. Well, I thought, if it means that much to them, I'll get the damn thing back, one way or another. Providing I can manage to stay alive.

I waited on the porch for several minutes, hoping that Laura would come out. But she didn't. After a while I stepped off the porch and headed toward town. There was quite a crowd around the saloon when I got there.

Kate Masters was standing just inside the batwings when I went in. She took my arm and said, "What are you after, anyway? Don't you know this is a game you can't beat?"

I half-smiled at her. The swelling in her face was beginning to go down, and, for some reason, she had stopped putting that rice powder on her face.

Without that flouncy costume, she would look pretty much the same as any other girl. I patted her shoulder, the way a man might pat a homeless dog.

"Don't worry about me."

"I can't help it. If it wasn't for me, you'd never have Jay down on you."

"Don't you believe it. You had nothing to do with it."

Something happened to her face. Those lively eyes became suddenly empty. "Oh," she said, and I knew then that she had heard the rumor about me and Laura Carney. I didn't know just how I had managed to slip into Kate Masters' life. Maybe she was just looking for another man, now that McCain had thrown her away. Or maybe she felt indebted to me for stepping in when McCain was knocking her around. Whatever it was, I didn't want to get mixed up with her any more than I already was. It was impossible to keep two girls as different as Kate and Laura locked up in one mind. So Kate had to go.

I grinned at her, with my mouth only. "You'd better get the bank. It looks like McCain's ready to go." Several idlers were beginning to come inside and the bar was getting a good play, even at that time of morning.

Before Kate turned to go, she said, "You know that poker won't settle this, don't you?"

"Yes, I guess I do."

"Jay is much better with a revolver than he is with his fists. Don't forget that."

"Thanks. I won't."

"And don't let Slim Kasper get behind you."

I nodded, and after a moment she went over to the bar and began to prepare the cigar-can bank. McCain and Kasper were sitting at a table near the wall, not saying anything, just sitting there, Kasper looking as though he would drop off at any moment. Denfield, I thought, you've played a lot of poker, but you've never got yourself into an affair just like this. I saw the Marshal—Silas Mills, his name was—leaning against the bar, not liking any part of what he saw. Still, there was no law against gambling. After a moment he walked over to me, his eyes a study in sobriety.

"That's a fine face you've got," he said dryly.

I said nothing.

"It's nothing to what you're apt to get, foolin' with McCain."

"Is there any law against gambling?"

"Don't get smart with me," he said harshly. "People didn't hire me as marshal just for bluff. If this thing gets to be any more than just gamblin', it'll be the end of both of you, and I'll see to it personally.

"There's something else you'd better know," he said, "and then I'm through. The story has it that McCain killed a man in Kansas, and one up on the Brazos. Self-defense both times. That's somethin'

101

you better think about, if you figure on stayin' on in Sabina." He looked at me with those hard, steellike eyes. "So far as I can prove, McCain's never broke a law here in Sabina."

Then he turned and walked heavily back to his place at the end of the bar.

I stood there for a moment, trying to figure it out. It was obvious that Marshal Silas Mills hated McCain, but, so far, he hadn't been able to do anything about it. The Marshal, in his blunt way, had tried to tell me several things. First, he had warned me that McCain was a killer and an expert gunman. He had killed two men and apparently had been freed both times on a plea of self-defense. That meant that he had deliberately let those two men draw on him before he had gone after his own gun.

I had the feeling that the Marshal had given me his blessing, in a left-handed sort of way—not that it was apt to do me much good. I glanced in his direction and he was staring darkly at Kate Masters. After a moment I went back to the table.

McCain said nothing. He bought his chips from Kate and I did the same. Kate fanned the cards on the table and he cut a nine of clubs and I cut the jack of hearts. I shuffled, he cut, and then I began to deal. I thought: River-boat poker was never like this. Bucking heads is never any way to gamble, but that was the way it had to be done now. Why don't you just cut high card with him and get it over with? I thought. Looking at him across the table, I couldn't help wondering if Laura would really have gone through with it. Would she have married him?

Most women would back away from a proposition like that, when all the chips were down. But I couldn't see Laura backing away from anything. She was a Carney, and I had learned by now that Carneys weren't like other people. It was frightening, in a way, the things they would do. To themselves. To others. Even now, with McCain in front of me, I could close my eyes for a moment and Laura would be there. I could hear her begging me to save her, when her own iron-hard will kept her from saving herself. I could almost feel the softness and warmth of her as she clung to me. The fire of her kiss.

That hand, with a ten in the hole and one showing, I bet into a pair of eights. McCain turned up a third eight from the hole. Denfield, I told myself, it's time to set your mind to poker.

It didn't do much good. McCain took three hundred dollars out of the kid's leather pouch that day. And he did it without cheating.

Chapter Six

I was tired, and completely disgusted with myself. Unless you have pored over cards for fourteen or fifteen hours without a letup, then you can't have any idea how hard a job gambling can be. I stood on the plank walk in front of the saloon, my muscles quivering with fatigue, my mind almost numb, dreading the moment when I would have to start walking toward the Charleston House. What would I say to Phil? What would I say to Laura? "I'm sorry, but it looks like Jay McCain is just a better poker player than I am." That would be fine. I could see their faces.

I wasn't worried about the kid. He would get that ranch back, one way or another, because he had absolutely no scruples to hold him back. And besides, I didn't care a tinker's damn about that ranch. But Laura—she was something else. I couldn't forget her, even for a moment, and I knew instinctively that that was the reason I had lost to McCain that night. I couldn't put my mind on poker. Every time I held a face card, there was Laura looking at me with those pleading eyes. How could I go back and tell her that I couldn't beat McCain?

Until now, the word "love" hadn't entered my mind in connection with Laura. But there had to be *some* explanation for their particular kind of insanity, and I guessed that love was it. It was even more powerful than the dream had been. Dreams do not have warm bodies and moist lips. You cannot reach out and touch a dream, and hold it in your arms. I thought bitterly: Oh, the dream has exploded, all right!

But how could I tell her that I had failed? How could I convince her that her brother was old enough to look out for himself? After all, who had lost the ranch in the first place? Let him tangle with McCain and get his fool self killed, for all I cared!

But I guessed she didn't figure it that way. How would I know how she felt about her brother? How could I know how she felt about anything, for that matter? Until two days ago she had been nothing but lies and a picture in a locket.

With those thoughts drifting in and out of my mind, I stood outside the saloon, not wanting to face Laura and too tired to figure out anything else to do. McCain and Kasper had drifted down the street to the hotel where they stayed. They were confident now. McCain was sporting a thick, meaningful grin. They would take care of this stranger, this tinhorn river-boat gambler. They would send him on his way in style, as soon as they got his money. Right out to the town cemetery, if they had anything to say about it. I stood there. The town was dark, practically deserted. Then the saloon door opened and Kate Masters came out.

"Oh," she said. "I thought you'd be gone by now."

I made a sound that was supposed to be laughter. "The pouch isn't empty yet."

"Jay just had a run of luck tonight. You'll make it up tomorrow." She looked at me, and then looked down. And because I didn't want to be alone right then, I said:

"Do you mind if I walk with you around to your place?"

If she minded, she didn't say so. She began moving up the plank walk and I fell in beside her, and we walked in silence until we got to her shack.

"Thank you," she said. "Good night." And she stood there very straight, with that ridiculous shack at her back. "If you want to come in for a while," she said, almost as an afterthought, "I can make some coffee."

It sounded better than going back to the Charleston House. So I went in. She lit the lamp and shook the coals in the stove and put coffee on to boil, and I sat on the bed watching her. "Do you mind if I ask a question?" she asked.

"Not at all."

Her voice became suddenly bitter. "What has Laura Carney got that men think is so fine?"

It is unusual to find a woman with such

directness, and the question startled me for a moment. Finally I said, "I wish I could tell you, but I'm afraid I can't. All I can say is that she's different from any woman I ever knew. She must be the only one of her kind in the world."

"Are you in love with her?"

"Yes—I guess I am." That was the kind of person Kate Masters was. You could tell her anything that came into your mind and it didn't seem to make any difference. Still, I marveled that I had said it. I hadn't completely admitted it to myself.

"So is Jay in love with her," she said, still working with the stove. "It's funny, in a way." But she didn't laugh. "All Laura Carney has to do is crook her finger and men trample each other to do her bidding. Is it because she sets herself up as such a lady? Well, she's not the only lady in Sabina. And she isn't beautiful, although she can make men think she is, it seems. What is it about her?"

"I told you, I don't know."

Then suddenly, "What is it between her and Jay? I know she wouldn't even look at a man like Jay McCain if she didn't have her reasons."

I was surprised that she didn't know. But, now that I thought about it, it made sense that McCain wouldn't want it to get around that he had to blackmail a girl into marrying him. So I told Kate Masters what I knew. Why I did it, I'm not sure,

107

except that she was easy to talk to and I knew it would never go any farther than the shack. When I got through, she laughed. She turned and faced me for a moment, and then she threw her head back and filled the room with shattering laughter.

"I didn't realize the story was that funny," I said.

"It's funnier than you know!" she managed to say when she got her breath. And then suddenly the laughter was over. She stood with her back to the lamp, making a long, distorted shadow across the floor of the shack. She looked very tired. She looked like a fifty-year-old child. "Yes, it's very funny," she said flatly, and then she took off the coffeepot and poured coffee into thick mugs. I moved over to the cook table and sat there waiting for the coffee to cool, waiting for Kate Masters to go on.

Finally she sat down at the table, looking around at the shabby room. "Saloon girl!" Her voice was harsh.

"How did you come to get mixed up with McCain, anyway?" I said.

"How does a girl ever get mixed up with a man? When I came to Sabina I was all alone, and McCain gave me a hand and got me a job with Stella in the saloon. He said it was just temporary and he'd find something better later. He didn't tell me that once a girl has worked in a saloon, all other jobs are closed to her. But I didn't care then. Jay kind of took the place of my father, I guess.

He was something to lean on. And he was the only man besides my father who ever gave me presents." She looked at a silver bracelet on her left arm, and suddenly she tore it off and hurled it across the room.

I was ready to let it drop, but she seemed in the mood to talk. If she wanted to get it out of her system, the least I could do was listen. I said, "Why was McCain so anxious to have you working in the saloon?"

She laughed again, that ugly sound. "I thought at first that he just wanted to help me, but I learned the real reason soon enough. I was younger than Stella or the other girls, and maybe prettier. It was my job to pick out the men with money and get them in the game that Jay and Slim Kasper kept going most of the time. Men are fools, most of them, and it wasn't hard." She looked at me, then down at her untouched coffee. "You're wondering why I kept it up, I guess. Well, there's not much choice for a saloon girl. Either she goes upstairs with the customers, or she drinks watered-down wine at a nickel a glass, and helps with the gambling. That wasn't the only thing, though. Until Jay hit me, I guess I thought I was in love with him, or maybe it was just that I so desperately wanted a fresh start. He said he'd marry me and take me to Kansas."

She spread her hands on the table, staring at nothing. "And I believed him. It just goes to show that women can be fools too, the same as men."

She seemed to be through talking. We sat there, letting the coffee get cold, and my mind kept drifting back to Laura Carney. What was I doing, sitting here with a fancy girl? I stood up and she said, "Do you think you can beat Jay at the poker table?"

"I don't know."

"I saw the cut you made, and the spread ace. He has a lot more tricks, better than that one."

"I figured that."

She looked at me, leaning heavily on the table. "Just one more thing," she said as I turned for the door. "McCain has his mind set on marrying Laura Carney. When he came to this town four years ago he was nothing. Now it's different. He has money, he has property. The only thing he doesn't have is respect—but he figures to get that by marrying a Carney."

"I'm not interested in McCain's private life," I said.

"You'd better be," she said flatly. "McCain was running when he hit Sabina. From the Army, from the law—it doesn't make any difference who he was running from. The thing that matters is that he has found a place where he can stop, and he's going to stay here."

"Maybe."

"I saw you talking to the Marshal today," she went on. "Silas Mills is a good man, but even he hasn't been able to get Jay out of town. McCain will run this town someday. He might even run the Marshal. Have you ever wondered what would happen if he killed you?"

"I haven't let myself dwell on it."

"Nothing would happen to him. It would be self-defense, the way it was with the other men he killed. No matter what the Marshal said, McCain could produce witnesses to prove his point. And no local jury would convict a local man for killing a stranger." She spread her hands again in a gesture of hopelessness that I had come to expect. "In the river country maybe you were good enough to take care of yourself, but this isn't the river country. There's no law down here except Silas Mills, and he can't do it all."

"What is it that you're trying to tell me?"

"It's simple enough," she said flatly. "Leave Sabina."

Everybody wanted to get me out of Sabina, it seemed, except Phil and Laura Carney. And they had their own peculiar reasons for wanting me to stay. I said, "Well, good night, Kate. I'll see you tomorrow."

"Sure. And the next day. Until McCain takes all your money."

I reached for the latch and suddenly Kate Masters was up from the table. "Jeff, don't you understand what I've been trying to tell you? The Carneys aren't worth the chances you're taking for them.

They're selfish and greedy and blown up with their own importance. Laura Carney's not for you. Let McCain have her, if that's what he wants. He would be getting no more than he deserves." Now she had her arms around my neck, and I stood there like a statue. "Jeff, can't you see that they're using you?"

I couldn't think of anything to say. While Laura was waiting for me, I had a saloon doxie hanging onto my neck. I felt a little sick.

"Jeff, leave Sabina. Go back to the country you know, to the people you understand." Her face was on my chest, and still I stood like wood. "Jeff, take me with you!"

I couldn't make a sound. I felt her stiffen against me, and slowly her arms came loose from my neck and she seemed to shrink away from me. "I didn't mean that," she said tightly. "I'm sorry." And she made a meaningless little gesture and turned her face away. "You . . . you'd better go."

I was sorry that I had hurt her, but it was too late for that. I heard myself mumbling something, and then I opened the door and went outside. Only when I was in the clean night air did the bitterness really hit me. For one violent moment I hated everything and everybody. Goddamn you! Who I was cursing, I didn't know.

The circumstances, maybe, that could land a girl like that in a saloon and make her what she was.

The self-righteous citizens of Sabina, who would not allow her a second chance.

Jay McCain.

Myself.

Who are you, Denfield, I thought, to accuse others of being self-righteous! Full of anger, I headed back toward town, deliberately taking the short cut where the beating had occurred, half hoping that they would try it again. I was in the mood to kill somebody. Anybody would do.

But nothing happened. As I turned in at the Charleston House I was relieved to see that the house was dark except for our upstairs room, where Phil was probably waiting. There was no one on the porch. Laura hadn't waited up, and I was glad of that.

I was surprised at the way the kid looked as I came in. His face was dirty and streaked with sweat, and his hickory shirt had white salt stains across the back and under the arms. He looked as if he had been doing a lot of riding. He lay across the bed, fully clothed, only grunting as I came in.

"Did you go out to the ranch today?" I asked.

"I rode out that way. How did the game go?"

"Not good." I sat on the edge of the bed, feeling wrung out and lifeless. "McCain's tough. He took three hundred off me today, and if I keep playing with him he's apt to take it all."

"It's my money. I'm not afraid of your losin' it.

If I'd been afraid of that, I'd never have brought you to Sabina." Then he sat up and looked at me. "What's the matter, Jeff? I'm not losin' faith in you, if that's what's botherin' you."

That was just the trouble. If he hadn't had so much blind faith in me, it wouldn't have been so bad. "Besides," he said, "it's the only chance I've got of gettin' that ranch. I won't allow Laura to marry McCain, I'll kill him first."

But I wasn't listening. As I looked out the window, I saw something in the yard in front of the boardinghouse, something white, as pale as a ghost in the moonlight. It was Laura.

"Where're you goin'?" Phil Carney said.

"Down to get some air. I'm too wound up to sleep."

There's no explaining some of the things I do. First, I was hoping to miss her; now a few minutes later it seemed just as important that I see her.

She made a small, startled sound as I came through the front door. She was just standing there, at the bottom of the porch steps, looking off to the west somewhere—or maybe she was just looking at the darkness. I saw then why she looked so pale and ghostlike. She was wearing only her night-gown and a white cotton wraparound. Another woman would have screamed, probably, if a man had come upon her like that, but not Laura Carney. After she made that small sound of surprise, she

114

turned to me and smiled very faintly. "It's too hot inside to sleep," she said. "I often come out here on nights like this."

I hadn't noticed the night being especially hot, but I didn't mention it now. She came up to the front porch, her feet bare. Her dark hair had been loosened from that tight bun at the nape of her neck, and now it flowed like jet silk over her shoulders. If there had been any questions in my mind, there were none now.

"This country is beautiful at night," she said. "It's wild, but all wild things have a certain kind of beauty to them. Jeff, have you ever seen a sea of brush when the moon is high?"

"No. I guess not."

"It's like an etching in silver. But you don't like this country do you?"

"I don't know much about it."

Where the words came from, I don't know. I stood there staring at her, and she would say something and someone would answer her with my voice. All I thought about was her, and I didn't even know what she was talking about.

"This is the only country I know," she said. "And I love it." A faint breeze came up and strands of her dark hair lifted gently as she turned toward it. "Do you smell the sage? At nights I can always smell it, even in town."

I caught the scent now, and there was a wildness in it. If they made a wild-sage perfume, it would be the kind for Laura Carney to wear. No picture in a locket was ever like Laura Carney.

"Jeff," she said. And then she turned and looked up at me, and my arms went out and closed around her. "Hold me close," she said, so softly that it was hardly a sound at all. And that sudden savagery took hold of me. I pressed my mouth onto hers and the fire blazed high, and only after several moments had passed did the flame begin to settle.

I had meant to say nothing, and I have no remembrance of the words coming from my throat. But I heard them. And the voice was mine. "I love you, Laura. I've loved you for a long time." Words hanging empty on the night air.

"I know," she said. "Phil told me part of it."

"It doesn't make sense," I said. "It makes no sense at all. You're not at all the way I had pictured you in my mind, but somehow that makes no difference. Do you think it's possible for a person to fall in love with an idea?"

"Yes, I believe that. And it works for women too, you know."

At first I didn't understand. I had pictured myself as running on a lonely, one-way track, going nowhere. I had refused to let myself believe that a person could *be* loved by an idea, a dream. Was that what she was trying to tell me?

She must have read my mind. She said, "Don't talk now. Don't ask questions." She clung to me and began shaking, and I knew then that she was afraid of something, really afraid. "Don't ask questions, Jeff. Please, don't."

I don't know how long we stood there. And finally she said, "Jeff, I'm glad you came to Sabina. I'm awfully glad." She looked up at me, and then down. I guess she could see that I was thinking about McCain. Would she really have married him? Would she still marry him, if my gambling luck didn't change?

After a while I said, "This is no good, Laura. I came to Sabina with the idea in my mind that I was going to set myself straight. I was going to cure myself of an obsession that went by the name of Laura Carney. Well, it looks like it didn't work. I'm worse off than I was in Virginia."

She only clung to me, and after a moment she said, "Don't talk now."

"I've got to talk. Ever since I got off the stage here everything has been wrong. A man I hardly know wants to kill me. I'm in love with a girl who's already engaged to another man. I'm involved in a gambling spree where there's nothing in the world for me to win."

"Nothing?" she asked quietly. "Nothing, Jeff?"

She pulled my face down until I could see the shining, metal-like flecks in her eyes. I could hear her breathing. I could feel her heart beating. I closed my eyes for an instant and her warm mouth touched mine, and I knew that I was lost. I

117

would continue to live in my own little private vacuum that I had made for myself.

"Nothing?" she asked again, after a long while. "What about McCain?"

She could never lie about McCain; the disgust was in her eyes. "I told you about him."

"But you were going to marry him just the same. You'll still marry him, won't you, if my poker playing turns out to be less than Phil expects?"

She stopped me in the only way she knew, with that moist, warm mouth of hers. "Jeff, don't ask me, because I don't know. I can't know until the time comes—if it does." Then, after a pause, she said, "Would you believe me if I told you I . . . loved you?"

That was the reason, I guess, that I'd insisted on talking. I wanted to drag it out of her, I wanted to hear her say it. And now that she had said it, I didn't know what to do. I could only hold her, feel the softness of her against me, and that only made me want her more. But that one big question kept coming back.

"What if I lose to McCain?"

She didn't have to say it. It was in her eyes, in the determined line of her mouth. It was a built-in decision. Ready-made. Long ago she had decided that the kid would get that ranch back and the Carney name would live on in Texas. That, to her, was more important than herself, or me, or anything else. That was the way Carneys were built. I couldn't change it, even if I wanted to.

And only then did it occur to me that I didn't want to change it. Take the steel out of her character and she wouldn't be Laura, she would be just another woman.

Long after Laura had gone back to her room, long after I went back to mine and lay wide-eyed and restless, I thought about it. For the first time in many months, I began to relax, and a queer sort of peace came down and settled there in the room. What are you stewing about? I asked myself. Within your reach is something that you didn't even think was real; within your reach is something every man dreams about but never gets. Not a woman, but *the* woman. No compromises, no bargain-counter shopping, no settling for less than what is absolutely right for you and for nobody else in the world. Think of it, Denfield. How many men do you know who married exactly the kind of women they wanted? None of them! And you know it! A thing like this doesn't happen every day, maybe not more than every century.

What you've been trying to do, I thought, is change her. That's the last thing you want to do, for she wouldn't be Laura any other way; not the Laura *you* want.

You couldn't break steel like her; and anyway, I wouldn't want her if she were broken, I wanted her just exactly the way she was, full of fire and slightly wild. No, I wouldn't try to change her.

Someday I might tame her, but that was different. You could tame a horse gently or you could break him with a club; there were different ways of doing everything.

And what are *you* going to do, Denfield?

I had known from the first what I was going to do, ever since that night in the Virginia peach orchard, so long ago. I was going to marry Laura Carney. I was going to be one man in a hundred million—I was going to marry *the* woman. If I had to win her in a poker game, that was all right with me. If I had to kill McCain, that was all right, too. I didn't even know if she loved me, or was using me, as her brother had suggested. Even at this point I hadn't become so addled that I believed everything she said. Still, that wasn't the important thing right now. The important thing was that I had found her and I wasn't going to let her get away.

And that's the way it's going to be? I thought.

There was no doubt about it. I could feel her. I could close my eyes and see her. There's only one cure for a thing like that, and that's possession.

Chapter Seven

One thing my coming to Sabina did was to increase Mrs. Lorring's boardinghouse business. The dining room was filled the next morning. There was little enough to gossip about in a town like that, and when a situation arose concerning two people like Laura Carney and Jay McCain, it was bound to bring them in. They were hoping that McCain and I would stop this fencing with poker and get down to shooting, and that morning their wishes were almost fulfilled.

It happened after the morning meal was over and most of the boarders were already heading toward town. I was waiting on the front porch for a chance to talk to Laura again when Phil Carney came out.

"Is McCain still in there?" I asked.

"And mad as hell," he said. "Laura just set him down again." Grinning, he began rolling a brown-paper cigarette. "You know, I'm beginnin' to believe that you're just the man to tame that sister of mine."

"What is that supposed to mean?"

He shrugged, holding a match to his cigarette, then changed the subject. "Will there be a game today?"

"That will be up to McCain, I guess. By the way, how can he spend so much time in town and still run a ranch?"

The kid laughed. "I guess he's afraid *not* to stay in town; it's the only way he can keep an eye on Laura. Anyway, the ranch more or less runs itself this time of year. The Indian agents won't be buyin' for another three months, so the gatherin' won't start till then." From the way he said it, I got the idea that he was already beginning to consider the beef gathering his job, just the way it had been when the ranch was his. That bottomless faith of his made me feel even more helpless than usual.

As we stood there, an idle thought got itself caught in my mind. I kept remembering the things Kate Masters had told me about McCain. I said finally, "I can see how a man could acquire position in this part of Texas by marrying a Carney. Do you think that's the reason McCain's gone to so much trouble to get the date set?"

The kid looked at me. I was vaguely surprised when he didn't laugh. "That may be part of it," he said.

"You think he's really in love with her?" I tried to make the question sound casual but still felt a bit ridiculous.

"In love with her?" He looked at me, then at his cigarette. "I don't know exactly what it means but I guess it's as good a word as any to describe what has happened to McCain. I've seen it happen to others, long before McCain. I never could understand it, but I guess that's because I'm her brother. When she was just a pigtail girl all she had to do was look at a man and she owned him."

He snapped his cigarette into the front yard, completely objective about it as he talked. "I know what it is to love a piece of land," he said. "A few ranch buildings, a few corrals, a herd of half-wild cattle. But I never loved a woman, so I wouldn't know how McCain feels about that. But look at it this way. If it's position he wants, he could get that by gettin' himself elected to office. Or he could make a play for some of the town girls here in Sabina. Most of them are as pretty as Laura. They all have more money, they don't have to work in boardinghouses for their room and board. That ranch gives him all the position a man could ask for. It makes him the biggest man in Sabina. So why should he deliberately put it on the block?"

It was a good question, and Phil Carney seemed to have answered it himself. Neither of us got the chance to give it further thought right then. We became aware of the voices. Angry voices.

Phil said, "It's Laura and McCain. They're still at it."

This was Laura's problem, I told myself. She'd got herself into it and it was up to her to get herself out. I was already inside the house by the time I thought it.

They were still in the dining room, everybody but Mrs. Lorring. McCain and Laura were standing with their faces almost together at the end of the dining table, yelling at each other. Mrs. Lorring was trying to get into the dining room from the kitchen, but Slim Kasper leaned lazily, half-smiling, against the doorframe, blocking the way. By the time Phil and I reached the room, Laura and McCain were shouting their anger. I knew something about Laura's temper, and McCain's too. It looked as if both of them had exploded at the same time.

Laura was saying, "It's none of your business; nothing I do is any of your business!"

"Then I'll make it my business! You're promised to me; it's all over town! Nobody's goin' to make a fool out of me, not even a Carney!"

Then Laura cut him off with a shattering burst of laughter. They were quite a match, a wildcat and a mad buffalo. Slim Kasper seemed to be enjoying it in that quiet, sardonic way of his, and even Phil Carney looked faintly amused. I found nothing amusing about it myself. I thought for a split second that McCain was going to hit her, as a matter of pure reflex, the way he had hit Kate Masters. But instead he grabbed her arm. It was like a matchstick being caught in a bear trap. The gambler's face was red, and beneath the red a bluish network of veins stood out on his forehead.

"Shut up!" he yelled.

If Laura felt any pain, it didn't show on her face or in her voice. She continued that nerve-grating burst of laughter, which was beginning to affect me as well as McCain. I don't remember crossing the room at all. I just remember grabbing McCain's shoulder, jerking him half around, and hitting him full in the face with my right fist.

If I had any idea of being a hero, of stepping in and ending it in a hurry with one blow, I forgot about it immediately. McCain blinked when I hit him. That was all. I should have hit him again, right then, before he had a chance to swing into action. But I didn't. I was too surprised. I had never seen a man take a blow like that and show no ill effects at all. I just stood there, not exactly scared, but full of the knowledge that it was going to be a very long morning. And a rough one.

I had somehow got the idea that because McCain hadn't gone for his gun that day in the saloon, he was basically a coward. I couldn't have made a worse guess. He was a careful man, but no coward. He didn't show his cards until the pot was counted, but that only meant that he was a good gambler. He had no scruples against bush-whacking a man in a dark alley, but the only thing that proved was that he liked to do things the easy way, whenever possible. But if he had to, he could do things the hard way. He was just about ready to show me how efficient he was at doing things the hard way.

He let go of Laura's arm and brushed her away, while I still stood there, losing my chance to take the edge off him. Now I had all that anger directed at me, all that anger that was aching to be turned loose on something. He was amazingly fast for a big man. He didn't say a word. He simply shifted his weight from the left to the right and hit me. I was watching that gun of his. I was thinking that maybe he figured now was the time to play all or nothing and try to rid himself of all competition permanently. While I was watching that gun he hit me.

I've never been hit harder. A fist loomed up as big as a ham and seemed to explode in that vulnerable, soft region just under the breastbone. The force of the blow seemed to punch my stomach up into my throat. I suddenly wanted to be sick. At that moment the thing I wanted most in the world was to be allowed to die quietly. But there was no time for that. The force of the blow sent me reeling back, crashing over the table and into chairs. I heard someone scream; maybe it was Laura. And then I was on the floor scrambling around in the wreckage, and McCain was crashing down on top of me with all fours.

I didn't want to move. It would have been nice just to have lain there, but that was a luxury that I couldn't afford. If I wanted to live I had to get out of the way, I had to keep McCain at a distance until I began breathing again. I kicked a chair in front of me and McCain hit it, and then we were all together on the floor, me, McCain, and the chair. What was left of the chair.

While we were floundering I grabbed McCain's arms and tried to hold them. It was like trying to hold a mountain grizzly, but somehow I hung on until the spasmodic retching stopped and I was able to drag some welcome air into my lungs. Then he broke loose. I kicked out with what strength I had in my legs, and this time I was lucky. I caught him in the belly, just above the waistline, and he grunted and fell back.

I had enough time to get to my feet, but so did McCain, and now we were more or less on equal footing again. He didn't waste time. He came at me like a mad bull. I side-stepped and clubbed him behind the head, but he caught me anyway, and we went crashing into the wall. I heard the sound of breaking glass and china, and a picture fell off the wall with a slightly louder crash, and somewhere in the midst of all the confusion and noise Mrs. Lorring was screaming for us to stop it. But nothing short of homicide could have stopped it then, and even Mrs. Lorring must have known that.

The dining room was a shambles. I was sorry about that, and I thought vaguely that I should never have started anything in the house. My friends in Sabina were few enough as it was, and it wasn't going to help any getting the landlady down on me, but there wasn't time to worry about it. McCain had found the target again. As we grappled along the wall he began slamming those rock-hard fists into my midsection again, and he might have ended it right there if he hadn't let his anger get the best of him. He wasn't satisfied with the damage he was doing with his fists; he broke it off and tried one savage kick aimed at my groin.

It would have worked if it had connected. I

wouldn't have walked for a month if the toe of that boot had connected where he was aiming it. It didn't connect, but it wasn't because his aim was bad; it was just because he was a little winded, the same as I was, and beginning to slow down. I was able to turn in time to catch the kick on my thigh, and even that was not pleasant. The sharp toe of his boot slammed into the long muscle between my knee and my hip, and the pain shot all the way to my skull. It wasn't pleasant, but at least it gave me a small advantage because the kick had thrown him off balance. I aimed for his face, but he was falling back and my aim went astray and my fist caught him just below the chin, just about where his Adam's apple should have been.

When I saw his mouth fly open I thought that would be the end of it. His mouth was working, the color had drained from his face, and he had to grab the doorframe to keep from going down. He was the one who was hurt this time. He was the one whose lungs were beginning to scream for air and whose constricted throat wouldn't let any in. Knowing that I had hurt him gave me a savage satisfaction, because now I was remembering that night in the alley and that pistol whipping that he and his partner had served up for me.

I must have thought about it too long. I didn't think I did; I was under the impression that I was bearing in all the time with both fists and it was just a matter of seconds before he would be down for good. But he got out of it somehow. Still holding onto the doorframe, he shoved himself away from the wall, and out of the dining room. He crouched low, hunching those thick shoulders of his and pulling his head in like a kicked terrapin, and all I could find to hit was the meaty part of his upper arms and the iron hardness of his skull.

We were in the parlor now, and I was glad that the room was practically empty, because we were all over it. I was beginning to lose my enthusiasm for the fight. My arms were heavy and the salty taste of blood was in my mouth, and I was beginning to have trouble remembering what had started the fight in the first place. But McCain was just beginning to get his second wind. He straightened up suddenly. The tight line of his mouth didn't move, but I somehow got the idea that he was grinning. Then he hit me and I began to fall.

I fell halfway across the room and against the wall. And then we stood spread-legged, trading blows. The only thing that kept me going now was the memory of that night in the alley. We fought our way across the room and finally through the front door and onto the front porch. McCain stumbled once, fell off the porch, and landed on his back on the packed clay of the front yard. But he was up again by the time I got to him. Through a red haze I could see that the others had followed us out to the front porch. Mrs. Lorring had hold of Laura's arms and Laura was trying to get away but couldn't.

That was when I saw McCain glance toward the porch and nod. I followed the gambler's glance and saw Slim Kasper staring at me with those cool eyes of his. He was going for his revolver.

You don't have a lot of time to think it over when you see a man looking at you like that and going for his revolver. Instinctively I began grabbing for my own gun, but before I could make the move I heard Phil Carney saying:

"Don't try it, McCain."

For a moment the picture froze just the way it was, like one of those stilted, elaborately posed pictures that traveling photographers take at a half dollar a throw. I don't know when the kid had pulled, but he had his revolver in his hand and it was leveled directly at McCain. My hand was about halfway to my holster, and Slim Kasper's hand was already gripping the wooden butt of his own gun. Only after I had seen everything else did I finally realize that McCain had made a play for his gun. When the picture was snapped, when Phil Carney had closed the shutters with those warning words of his, McCain already had his revolver half out of his holster.

I didn't understand it at first, but it didn't take

long. It was quite a trick, better than spread aces any day. The timing was just about perfect, or would have been if it hadn't been for Phil Carney. McCain and Kasper must have practiced it plenty to get it down so perfectly.

This is the way it went—or the way it should have gone: The thing that pulled the trigger on the trap was that single insignificant glance and nod of McCain's. Ninety-nine times out of a hundred no one but the man he was fighting would notice such a small thing—but, lucky for me, this happened to be the one-in-a-hundred time. Phil Carney had seen it. Anyway, that one small action, in the midst of big action, was the thing that was supposed to make the trick work. McCain knew that I would follow that glance of his because I was watching everything he did. He was betting that I would act on pure instinct, and I had. He was also betting that instinct would make me go for my gun when I saw that Slim Kasper was about to pull, and he had been right.

That was where the trick of the thing really went to work. The whole thing was happening so fast that nobody was supposed to see that move of Kasper's but me. All they would see was me, a man who had decided to quit fighting with his fists and go for his gun. It all would happen so fast that it would never occur to anybody that Kasper was in it at all. I was fighting McCain, not Kasper. I was drawing on McCain; or that's the way it would look, and that's the way it would sound in a courtroom, after the funeral.

But, in that split second, I forgot about McCain completely. All I could see was that gun hand of Kasper's making its move. Kasper was the only man I was supposed to see, and that was what pulled the string. While I'd be trying to get in position to face this new attack, McCain would be pulling his own revolver and exploding a cartridge or two where they would do the most good.

It was all very neat, and not nearly so complicated as it sounds. After the smoke cleared, all anyone could say was that I had tried to draw and McCain had beaten me.

Self-defense.

A sudden rage, a brand-new rage, the kind of rage that I had never known before, took hold of me. Self-defense! Now I could understand about those two killings that McCain was credited with. They had been self-defense too!

For a small part of a second time seemed to have stopped. Now it exploded into life. All chances of gunplay were over; Carney had seen to that. McCain came at me again, charging head down like a wild buffalo. I didn't try to get out of the way. We met head on like two freight wagons, and for a long while I was oblivious of everything but the giving and taking of pain. It ended only when a giant hand took hold of me and hurled me, almost carelessly, against the porch railing. The same hand grasped the sleeve of McCain's shirt, jerked him around, and shoved him savagely to the ground.

The hand belonged to Marshal Silas Mills. It couldn't have belonged to anyone else.

Chapter Eight

Sabina's jail was a blockhouse affair next to the Marshal's office at the other end of town, near the wagon yard. Silas Mills marched McCain and me right through the middle of town, with most of the citizenry following behind. It must have been a strange parade. McCain and I were in about the same condition, our clothing in rags, our faces bloody, our legs too weak to hold us up—but the Marshal kept us walking anyway. He cursed us every step of the way and threatened to kill us with his own hands if we didn't keep walking, and maybe he would have.

Anyway, he kept us walking. We staggered like drunken bums, and once in a while one of us would stumble, but we'd get up. We were too exhausted to talk, too exhausted to do anything. I never thought that I'd be glad to be locked in a jail, but the only thing I felt was relief when we reached that one. I stumbled inside and heard the barred door clang shut, and I sprawled out on the uncovered plank bunk and concentrated for a long

133

while on not being sick. Concentrated on getting my heart to beating right again, on getting enough air into my scorched lungs.

Where McCain was, I didn't know, and at that moment I didn't care. I just lay there. In the background I could still hear the Marshal cursing, and I could hear the curious crowd milling around the jail, but I was completely uninterested in anything or anybody but myself. I had never been in a fight just like that one. I hoped I'd never be in another.

After a while I heard Phil Carney talking to the Marshal and the Marshal was still cursing, and I was still too completely exhausted to be interested in anything Phil Carney might be saying. Oh, this is a fine town, I thought bitterly. Just the kind of town for a war-weary veteran to come to, just the place for a good long rest.

That had been a very neat trick of McCain's, that self-defense trick of his. As neat and deadly as a new dirk. What kind of man would try a trick like that, what kind of man would go to all the trouble to work it out? A coward? No, McCain was a lot of things that I didn't like, but he was no coward. A sure-thing gambler, that's the kind of man that would rig up a trick like that and make it work.

The jail door opened.

"By God," Phil Carney said, "you're a mess."

"I feel a mess."

"Get up," he said. "We're goin' back to the Charleston House."

"You're crazy. I'm in jail. The Marshal went to a lot of trouble to get me here."

"Just the same, we're goin' back to the Charleston House. McCain's not filin' charges, and I told the Marshal you weren't either. So all we have to do is pay a fine for disturbin' the peace and you're free to go."

"And McCain?" I asked.

"He's already out. Kasper picked him up in a livery hack and they headed toward the ranch. McCain doesn't look any better than you do."

That wasn't much consolation. "That was a pretty fancy rig McCain fixed for me back there. How did you come to see through it?"

"I didn't see through it. I was just prepared for it. I know McCain and the things he'll try. When the fight started I just got my gun out and kept it ready."

It paid to be suspicious in Sabina. It paid not to trust anybody; I'd learn that someday, maybe. "Well," I said, "thanks anyway. But I don't know what I'm thanking you for. If it hadn't been for you, I wouldn't have come here in the first place."

The kid laughed. "You're all right. I wasn't sure at first."

I still wasn't sure. One of my eyes was beginning to swell shut, the whole side of my face was sore, and the inside of my jaw felt as if it had been loosely shaped from a package of dog meat. Later, when I could afford the luxury, I'd begin

135

to get mad again. But not now. I was too tired. "Are you sure the Marshal's going to let me out of here?"

"I'm sure. I've already paid the fine."

With a bit of effort I stood up. I picked up my hat, but before I could leave the cell Silas Mills had blocked the way. He was not so much bigger than McCain, he just looked that way, and he also looked mad. "Denfield," he said, "if I had my way I'd let you rot here, but lucky for you, I'm just the marshal here, not the judge and jury."

"And what would you do to McCain," I said, "if you had your way?"

It was the wrong thing to say, but at that moment I didn't care. At the mention of McCain, Silas Mills's face got almost purple. He didn't like McCain, and he was beginning to like me even less. "Get out," he said hoarsely. "I'll take care of McCain in my own way, Denfield, and that's one thing you'd better understand if you plan to stay in Sabina."

It was a long trip back to the Charleston House, but not so long as the one to the jail had been. There was quite a crowd around the jail waiting to see what I looked like, and when they were sure that I wasn't any better off than McCain, they seemed satisfied.

"What do they want?" I said. "What are they hanging around for?"

Phil Carney grinned faintly. "You don't under-

136

stand how dull a town like Sabina is most of the time. They're just curious, that's all. This is the first real excitement they've had in months."

We were passing the feed store now and there was quite a group of them, watching us silently. "Tell me something," I said. "Why do they hate me, anyway?"

"They don't hate you personally, they just don't like strangers. Besides, you told them your home was in St. Louis, and anywhere north of Red River is considered Yankee country down here."

"Good Lord," I said. "Didn't I put in three years with Hood, the same as you?"

But it was no use. I think even Phil Carney considered me slightly strange because I happened to be born somewhere besides Texas, so I couldn't very well expect the others to like me. Of course, McCain wasn't a native of Sabina either, but then, the citizens had had several years to get used to him. To hell with them, I thought. The stage office looked tempting as we passed it. All a man had to do was step up and say, "I want a ticket on the next stage north," and that would be the end of it. The end of everything. Even Laura.

And that was the reason I didn't do it.

It had been a long day, the longest day I'd ever tried to live through, and it wasn't even half over. The sun said it was about ten in the morning and the streets of Sabina were already hotter than the third level of hell, which didn't make me feel any better. Laura and Mrs. Lorring were standing on the front porch as we neared the Charleston House. It occurred to me that Mrs. Lorring wasn't going to enjoy seeing me at all, since I was the one who had started the fight in her dining room. But I forgot about that as Laura called, "Jeff, Jeff!" She came off the porch and flew down the path and the first thing I knew she was in my arms.

It was the first time she had shown any affection at all in public. Come to think of it, it was just about the first time I had seen her when she hadn't been mad at something. "Jeff, are you all right?"

"I'm fine. Not very pretty, maybe, but most of the damage will wash off with water." I liked having her in my arms, but still, it wasn't exactly a comfortable position for a man to be in, with so many looking on. I noticed that Phil Carney looked surprised, as though he had never seen his sister behave like this before and did not know what to make of it.

"Are you sure, Jeff? Are you sure you're all right?"

"I'm sure," I said. Mrs. Lorring was holding a broken china plate in one hand and looked as though she were about to cry. I didn't know what to say to her, so I didn't say anything. Phil Carney and I left the two women in the front parlor and went up to the room.

When I looked in the mirror I got a shock. I'd figured that my face wouldn't be much to look at, but somehow I hadn't expected that ugly, pulpy mass that looked back at me from the glass.

"I'll get some water," the kid said.

What I needed was a new face. It didn't seem possible that water could help the one I had. I lay across the bed for a few minutes while Carney plundered around in the kitchen looking for medicine and water. How long had I been in Sabina, anyway? Days? Weeks? It seemed more like centuries, or at least several lifetimes. If I stayed much longer the storekeepers were going to have to get in a new supply of healing salve and bandages.

It occurred to me then, for the first time, that there was a good chance that I had ruined everything. I couldn't very well see me and McCain sitting down to a game of poker after what had happened. A situation like this could go just so far before it reached the breaking point—and I had a feeling that the point had been reached about two hours ago in Mrs. Lorring's dining room. Winning a ranch over a poker table was a wild-eyed scheme to begin with, but it was the only one we had. And now that was gone. . . .

About that time Phil Carney came back in the room with water and salve and sticking plaster. He must have seen that something was wrong.

"What's the matter?"

"I was just thinking we're right back where we started."

"What are you talking about?"

"I can't see myself carrying on this poker fight with McCain after what happened this morning—although I probably would. During the past few days I've proved that I'm fool enough to try anything. But not McCain."

"Like hell he won't." The kid set the water on the dresser. "Why do you think he decided to gamble with you in the first place? Because he needs the money. McCain may own a ranch, but that doesn't mean that he's a rancher. He needs that two thousand dollars of yours to hold him over until the Indian agents start buying again. That's why he decided to gamble with you instead of kill you. And that's why he'll be coming back for more poker. He may not like it, but he'll be back, all right. He has to have that money."

"He could borrow it at the bank, couldn't he?"

"Sure he could, but he won't. That would make him look like a failure as a rancher, and McCain is a man who can't stand to be a failure at anything. Remember what I said once about hurting a man like that—the only way to do it is through his pride. That's another reason he'll be back. McCain never quits loser at anything."

Phil Carney's faith hadn't swerved a fraction of a degree. He was like some general, slightly withdrawn from the field of battle, a general who had all the information he needed charted neatly on his maps, and he was the only man in the midst of all the noise and confusion who felt that he actually knew how the thing would end. Generals don't always guess right, no matter how much information they have, but there was no use reminding Phil Carney of this. He had his faith.

Chapter Nine

For the next two days there was a great deal of suppressed excitement in Sabina as the word began to get around that the fight had settled nothing and that McCain would soon be coming back to pick it up where we'd left off. But he hadn't come back yet, and the waiting was beginning to get on my nerves. Which was what McCain had intended, maybe. I had no place in the town and served no purpose there, and soon I began to get restless and edgy, even with Laura.

It was about nine that night, a long while after supper, and I stood at the end of the Charleston House's front porch looking past the scattering of orange-lighted houses at that bleak brush country that completely surrounded the town. Every day I seemed to hate it more, and every day my longing for the lushness of the river country grew stronger.

Well, why don't you go, Denfield? Why don't you just pick up your blanket roll and leave?

"Jeff," Laura called from the front door, "are you out there?" That was why I didn't leave. That dream of mine had been a plaything for children compared to this, the real thing.

"Yes," I said, and she came out and stood there beside me. We hadn't spoken of McCain for several days. We pretended that we both had been born that night that she had said she loved me, and that nothing before that had ever happened. It wasn't a very satisfactory arrangement, and it wasn't very comfortable, but it was the only one that would do.

"The nights in this part of Texas are beautiful," she said. She had said it a hundred times, it seemed, as though she were trying to convince me that she was right. But it was different this time. She added, "You hate it, don't you, Jeff?"

"It's different from what I'm used to." That was as generous as I could be.

"What's the matter, Jeff?"

We knew what the matter was. Nothing was right for us and it seemed that it would never be right. That big question had grown bigger all the time in my mind, and it was seldom that I could think of anything else. Loving a woman was fine, and marrying was fine, but winning her in a poker game was something else again. The only worse thing that I could think of was losing her in a poker game. And it could be done. It *would* be done, if Jay McCain had anything to say about it.

"Jeff," she said, "is anything wrong?"

"Can't you guess?" I said, and I was suddenly angry.

She could guess, but that would be breaking one of our rules. The rule was that we never spoke of McCain. The rule was that we were never to look into the future. Well, I'm tired of rules, I thought. To hell with rules.

I took her shoulder and turned her toward me. "This is no good, Laura. It isn't natural and it just isn't any good."

She knew what I meant, and now she was angry too. "I'm sorry," she said, "but there's no way we can change it. If you don't like it . . ." Her voice trailed off.

"Laura," I said, "let's stop it. Let's get married and get away from here, away from Sabina, away from your brother and all the rest of it." I had forgotten for a moment that I had a personal score to settle here in Sabina. "Your brother's a man!" I almost shouted. "You can't take care of him always. You can't go on making sacrifices for him forever."

She looked at me as though I were talking in a strange language.

"Laura, don't you understand? It's just no good this way."

"You're the one who doesn't understand," she said flatly, with anger in her eyes. "You can't understand because you're not a Carney or a Texan, because you're not anybody but a river-boat gambler and you don't know what it means to have a family name to live up to, to be proud of."

I laughed, and the sound was ugly. "I'm not good enough for you, is that what you want to say? Well, why don't you go ahead and marry McCain? He's willing to co-operate. Your brother will get the ranch back and the Carney name will mean something again. If that's so important to you, then why don't you go ahead and do it?"

"Jeff!"

But I was wound up now and couldn't seem to stop. I knew it was senseless, but still I couldn't stop that angry flow of words once they had started. "Your father may have been a fine man," I said, "but that was because he was a man and not because he was a Carney."

"Phil and my father are of the same blood," she said stubbornly. "You can't change that."

"And Phil's a fool. You can't change that, either. If that ranch was so important to him, he had to be a fool to gamble it off in the first place."

"He was just a boy. Can't you understand that?"

"Boy!" The word sounded like a curse.

Her voice was suddenly calm, and very cold. "It's impossible for you to understand what that ranch means to Phil. But getting it back, working it, making it something big is my brother's way of paying a debt to himself."

"Debts are honestly paid only by one's own earnings."

"I don't expect you to understand."

"And I don't. But there's one thing I'd like to

know—does this ranch mean the same thing to you as it does to your brother?"

"No. It couldn't, because I wasn't responsible for losing it."

"Still, to get it back, you were willing to marry a man like McCain."

She said nothing.

"Why?" I demanded. "Is it just because he's your brother?"

"It's because he's the son of my father."

It made absolutely no sense, and we were right back where we started, and the only thing I had learned was that Carneys behaved like Carneys, and nothing, it seemed, could stop them. This land was in them, its violence and bleakness of soul and ruthlessness. I suddenly felt empty and defeated. How was a man to fight this land or the people that grew out of it?

"Jeff . . ." Her anger had been spent, and so had mine.

"Yes?"

"I'm sorry. I didn't mean all I said."

"You were right about part of it, I guess. I never had a family name to be proud of and I don't know what it's like."

"It's important to Phil that he become the man his father was. It's his life."

"Yes, I guess it is." For some reason, I remembered something the kid had said shortly after we had arrived in Sabina. I had forgotten the exact words, but I did remember that he had mentioned immortality, and the feeling a son had carrying on his father's work. "Maybe that's the only immortality we'll ever know—and if it is, it's good enough for me." It was strange that that bit of confession should occur to me. It hadn't meant much to me at the time, but now it seemed to give a kind of rhyme and reason to Phil Carney and to the drive that kept him going.

"Jeff, are you angry?"

"No. But will you answer a question for me? It isn't about McCain."

"All right."

"If things were different," I said, "would you marry me right now? Would you go with me to my own country and my own kind of people?"

Several long seconds must have passed before she finally answered, and I was glad that she had taken plenty of time to consider it. "Yes," she said at last. It was a question that I had been afraid to ask before, for I knew how much she loved this land. "Yes," she said again, strongly this time, as though in confirmation.

"Then everything will be all right," I said. And I believed it. It didn't occur to me until later that that blind, unswerving faith of Phil Carney's might be contagious.

I awoke early the next morning. It was dark outside and the kid was still asleep, but the women were already at work downstairs, in the kitchen. I sat up in bed and thought: This will be the day. I knew it. The edge of decision was on the air that morning.

This will be the day. The feeling hung on. I went downstairs and splashed cold water on my face at one of the washstands at the side of the house. Later, as I ate with the others in the battered dining room, I could see that Phil Carney began to feel it too. Then a visiting cowboy came in and seated himself near the end of the table. Helping himself to biscuits and sorghum, the cow hand spoke with labored casualness.

"I hear Jay McCain's in town. It's a pretty good ride from his place. He must of got an early start."

I glanced at Phil Carney, but not at Laura. This was the day, all right.

Chapter Ten

Stella's saloon was doing a brisk business that morning. The curious, the morbid, the hangers-on, they all stood hipshot along the bar as Carney and I walked in. All eyes turned on us, but my own gaze was directed toward the back of the place, where McCain and Kasper were waiting. This was the day, all right. McCain's battered face told me that much. There was a sharpness in his eyes that said that the sparring was over.

I felt someone touch my arm; it was Kate Masters. "Jeff, do you think you ought to be here?"

"I guess we'll know by sundown. What's McCain got on his mind? Does he want a showdown?"

She nodded.

"Well, I guess you might as well get the bank and a fresh deck." I turned to Carney. "Just to be on the safe side, you might keep an eye on Kasper for me. I've got a feeling that McCain is just about all I can handle today."

The men in the saloon were slowly closing in around us, as though they were afraid I would change my mind at the last minute and make a run for it. The kid touched my shoulder. "Good luck, Jeff." Then I sat down at the table and McCain and I looked at each other.

The gambler's face was as battered as my own, but there was little satisfaction to be taken from that. He looked well rested. He looked as though he were anticipating a long, long day ahead, and he was ready for it. I only hoped that I was as ready.

We didn't say a word until Kate Masters had the bank set up and a new deck opened. "Poker?" I said finally.

"Draw."

We cut for the deal and he got it. This is one day you'd better keep your eyes open, I thought, as he shuffled quickly, expertly. Jay McCain didn't come to town today just for another game of poker. He came to win. He came to settle this thing once and for all. I cut and anted, and then he began to deal. Two-handed draw. Hour in and hour out, I couldn't think of a worse game to play. Watch him, I kept telling myself. Watch every move he makes or you're lost.

The first pot was a small one and McCain took it with three of a kind. I hope that isn't an omen, I thought. Then I took the cards and wasn't very subtle about inspecting them. I turned them over and riffled them quickly, my eyes glued to the intricate scrollwork on the backs of the cards. They weren't marked. Even the slightest, most subtle change in that scrollwork would have jumped at me during the quick riffle. Well, that was one thing I didn't have to worry about. I blocked the deck and quickly studied the edges. No sign of crimping or nailing or smudging or any of the other hundred and one methods a cheater uses to gain an advantage.

McCain wasn't missing a bit of it. He cut carelessly, smiling the smallest smile in the world. He knew something that I didn't know, and I had no way of guessing what it was. There was no sign of worry in those eyes of his. He was going to win. As far as he was concerned, it was a dead certainty.

I felt myself sweating. It wasn't possible that a man could be so sure of himself unless he had a plan. Unless he had discovered a way to overcome the elements of pure chance and skill. I began to deal. You've just got to keep your eyes open, Denfield. You can't afford to even *blink* your eyes. Not while Jay McCain is across the table.

By midafternoon, what was supposed to have been a high-stake poker game had taken a strange turn; less than a hundred dollars had changed hands. McCain was playing sure-thing poker. Never taking chances, never bluffing, always playing percentages. If your bankroll is low, if you can be satisfied with a small winning at the end of a long day, then sure-thing poker is the thing to play. But not if you're out to take two thousand dollars from a man!

I couldn't figure it. Time after time the pot never got bigger than the original ante. If McCain wasn't sure that his cards were good enough to win, then he turned over and waited for another hand. On every deal I inspected the cards and they were scrupulously clean. It bothered him not at all that he had lost a few dollars by playing his cards too close. It even seemed to amuse him.

It didn't amuse me. If a man didn't want to bet his money, there was nothing much you could do about it. Toward sundown my shoulders began to ache, my back was getting stiff, and my head wasn't so clear as it had been a few hours before. When it came my deal I shoved the cards back to the center of the table.

"I've had enough. We'll take it up tomorrow, if you want to."

McCain straightened slightly, almost smiled. "We'll take it up right now, Denfield. You came to gamble. All right, we'll gamble until one of us is broke. That's what you want, isn't it?"

I was beginning to get it now. In a fight to the finish, McCain thought he could outlast me. That explained the close-to-the-vest game that he had been playing. A game like this could go on all day, all night—maybe even longer. As far as poker was concerned, we were evenly matched, and there wasn't much chance that either of us would get much ahead as long as McCain insisted on playing it close. But when one of us began to get groggy, that's when things would change, and McCain was betting that it would change in his favor.

I didn't like it. McCain knew too much about handling cards. And it's tough enough to catch a second dealer when you're wide awake and alert; practically impossible when you're numb for want of sleep. I pushed my chair back, signifying that the day's game was over.

"This is your last chance, Denfield."

"There's always tomorrow."

McCain shook his head, but he was looking at Phil Carney now, not at me. "There'll be no tomorrow. When this game's over, I'm through."

He was lying. I knew McCain would never rest until he broke me, one way or the other, but Phil Carney wasn't so sure. He could see his big gamble missing fire, he could see that ranch fading away, drifting out of his grasp. It wasn't in him to stand up to McCain's bluff.

"See it through, Jeff." The words were drawn tight. I knew that I'd never get up from that table without a big argument or fight, and the last thing I wanted was a scene like that. I sat there for a full half minute, feeling the resistance go out of me. What if McCain really meant it when he said this was my last chance? I had come a long way to have it end like that, like excusing myself from a tea party. And what the hell, I thought, it's the kid's money, it's his gamble . . .

I pulled my chair back up to the table, knowing that I had lost my first big hand, maybe the most important hand that I would ever lose. But I lost it. I took the cards and began to deal.

The good citizens of Sabina, who had at first been disappointed with the game, were now beginning to work up a healthy interest. They accepted it for what it was, an endurance contest, and from the grins on their faces I could see that they thought McCain had pulled another smart one. And I was afraid they were right.

As long as you have big pots, several men around the table to keep tabs on, it's not hard to keep interested in the game. But the monotony of a game like this was almost overpowering; the sameness of every hand played, the leanness of the pot began to work on my brain like morphine. I began to anticipate McCain's every move, I began to play my cards even before I had them fanned in my hand. It was the same thing over and over and the pot was so lean that it seemed to make little difference whether I won or lost.

I heard no sound from Phil Carney. In the background there was only the monotonous shuffling of the onlookers as they came, went, drank, ate, or just stood and stared, and the game dragged on and on. Toward midnight Stella had coffee made and brought it to the table. Kate Masters, McCain, and I drank without speaking, and the game continued. Stella made no move to lock the saloon. There was a subdued excitement around the table, apart from the drudgery of the game itself, that kept bringing the onlookers back and back again.

How long have I been sitting here? I wondered. I stared blearily at my spread cards and tried to count the hours in my mind. Sixteen or seventeen hours, at least, I figured. That wasn't so long. I had been in longer games, much longer, but never one like this, where nothing ever happened. How are you doing, McCain? Are you as tired as I am?

There was nothing in his face to tell me how he was doing. It was past midnight now and he didn't look so fresh as he had looked that morning, but whether he was as tired as I was, I didn't know. All right, goddamn you, I thought, we'll see how alert you are. I drew two cards to a pair of fours and a king and got no help. After McCain had drawn two cards, I bet the pot limit. McCain called without raising and showed three kings.

Three kings! And he hadn't done anything with them! Calling my bluff, just to keep the game even and monotonous as possible, but not raising! Well, that was the game he had set for himself, and he was sticking to it, I could say that much for him.

By now, I thought, I must be a classic study in frustration. It's a small, stupid game and McCain is determined to keep it a small, stupid game until he's damned well ready to make it something else, and there's not a thing I can do about it. I counted my chips and I was a little over a hundred dollars ahead, a fact that bothered McCain not at all. Outside the saloon, the chill of dawn was breaking over Sabina, and the chill got into my bones and ate at my nerves.

Most of our audience had drifted away by this time. There were two cow hands who probably had nowhere to sleep, Phil Carney, Stella, and Kate Masters. I couldn't tell what Phil Carney was thinking. His face was pale and drawn, and he hardly blinked as he watched the play hand after hand, hour after hour. Stella was shaking the wood stove, preparing more coffee, and Kate Masters sat like a statue at the table, guarding the bank, opening new decks when they were needed. Occasionally I would catch her staring at McCain, but mostly she looked at nothing. She sat with her hands folded, staring blankly at the green felt covering on the poker table.

Almost twenty-four hours we had been sitting there. A long day, and a long, long night, and God knew how much longer it would go on. There was nothing I could do to speed up the game. McCain had planted himself in the driver's seat, and he was going to stay there come hell or high water, his losses be damned.

If I was smart, I thought, I'd get up and get out of here. I'd tell McCain to go to hell, and Phil Carney, and all the rest of them, and I would go somewhere and get some sleep. What I did was drink more coffee while Kate Masters opened a new deck.

What surprised me most was that McCain had made no attempt at cheating. The cards, when they were taken from the game, were as clean as they had been in the sealed box. He hadn't even attempted to crimp the aces, an act that came as naturally as breathing to gamblers like McCain. He kept his hands on the table at all times. His shirt sleeves were rolled, discarding the possibility of a mechanical holdout. For reasons of his own, a crooked gambler was making a great show of his honesty.

I didn't know what his reasons were, but I had an uneasy feeling that I would find out before long. I only hoped that it wouldn't be too late.

Pretty soon our audience began drifting in again, and by noon the saloon was almost full. They knew it couldn't last much longer. Almost thirty-six hours the thing had been going on, and there was a limit to how long gamblers could stay awake.

It was about three in the afternoon when McCain decided to end it.

Both of us were groggy, stupid, half lame from sitting in one position so long, half blind from staring at the cards. Kate Masters had been there the whole time, and now she was sipping a glass of wine that she had bought out of the bank. It was my deal; I cut the deck, blocked the cards, and shuffled them thoroughly, automatically, my hands feeling as though they didn't even belong to me, but doing the work that they had been trained to do just the same. McCain cut carelessly. Then, as I blocked the cards for the deal, he said:

"All right, Denfield, now we'll see how much of a gambler you really are. You want that ranch of mine. That's the reason you came to Sabina, isn't it?"

This was McCain's play. I waited.

"That's what I thought," he said, and that slow, small smile touched the corners of his mouth. "I'm goin' to give you a chance to get what you came after. You have two thousand gold in the bank, plus some of my money. We'll play one hand for the bank. If you win, we'll play the bank against my ranch."

It took me a second to find my voice. "And if I lose?"

He grinned. "You leave Sabina for good. And you leave alone."

Kate Masters made a small, surprised sound. The wineglass dropped from her hand and she quickly took a scarf from her neck and wiped the liquid from the table. I glanced at Phil Carney and his eyes were alive and hot. He nodded.

My sluggish brain refused to work; I had only my instincts to warn me that something was wrong. It was a fair bet he was offering, parlaying two winning hands into ownership of the ranch. The odds were against my having two winning hands, of course, but they were fair odds, and that was the thing that bothered me. McCain wasn't the kind of man to offer fair odds; not when all the chips were down, the way they were now. I know him.

Still, I couldn't find anything wrong with it. The cards were clean. I had shuffled them myself and it was my deal. Not even McCain could practice cheating when he couldn't even touch the deck. Or could he?

In those few seconds, as Phil Carney silently urged me to take up the challenge, as the onlookers grumbled impatiently, as Jay McCain grinned with a self-assurance that was not natural, I managed to shake some of the sluggishness from my brain. Was it possible for a man to stack the deck without touching it? That was the thing I had to determine. I had never heard of such a thing, and I was sure that I knew every trick in the crooked gambler's

157

book. It was impossible! It absolutely had to be on the level, because I had shuffled the cards and would deal them myself. The only possible way McCain could rig the hand was to slip in a cold deck, with the top cards prepared to come off just the way he wanted them. And that was impossible, too, because McCain had never moved his hands from the table.

And then it hit me! *Kate Masters.*

She had spilled that wine at just the right time. After the shuffle. After the cut had been made—*but while the cards were still on the table!* With trained hands, it would have been simple enough to switch a prepared deck for the one I had shuffled, taking advantage of my exhaustion and sluggish reactions, using that scarf to hide the prepared deck and take out the other one, as she pretended to wipe up the spilled wine.

It could have happened that way. I had seen trained hands do it; I could do it myself.

It *could* have happened. But *did* it?

That was something that I had to let instincts decide, and my instincts said yes. I picked up the deck and thought I could see a touch of relief in McCain's eyes. I thought: Pay attention, McCain. I'm going to give you a lesson in outcheating a cheater. Are you ready?

I said, "The bet is made, McCain. This hand for the bank. Five cards, up or down?"

He shrugged. "You're the dealer."

Good. I would serve them down. I would let him have it all at once, fast, like a bullet in the head. Pay attention, McCain, this will be a lesson that you won't soon forget!

I dealt the first cards, one to McCain, one to myself, face down. My hands weren't working so automatically now, they felt a bit clumsy, and were a bit clumsy, because the ordinary gambler isn't called on to second deal every day in his life, and he gets a bit rusty. But not too rusty. That's something you forgot, McCain, part of your lesson. In self-protection, a professional gambler must learn the tricks of crooked gamblers. You won't forget that the next time, McCain. If there is a next time.

The five cards were dealt out—but with a difference. Holding the deck in my left hand, pushing the top card forward with the thumb of my left hand as if to deal it, then darting the thumb of my right hand in to pull out the second card. Second dealing. A clean, almost foolproof trick of crooked gamblers, but ordinarily used only with marked cards. I had found another use for it, dealing McCain the second card, the one meant for me, while I took the one meant for him. Now the hands were reversed. If Kate had actually switched decks, I now had the hand that she had prepared for McCain, and McCain had the hand that should have been dealt to me.

I had guessed right. I knew it the second McCain

picked up his hand and glimpsed his first card. Thunder was in those eyes of his. I spread my own cards on the table—three kings and two aces.

"Can you beat a full house, McCain?"

He looked as though he were choking. There was a hiss like escaping steam as the onlookers let out their breaths, and Phil Carney came to his feet as rigid as an oak beam.

"What have you got, McCain?"

There was murder in the big gambler's eyes, but not for me. Not now. And not for Phil Carney. He glared at Kate Masters, his throat swollen, his big hands twitching. Savagely he threw his hand to the floor.

"Now the bank against the ranch," Phil Carney said. "That's the deal he made, Jeff."

But I knew, and everyone else knew, that the game was over. There would be no more poker, ever, between me and McCain. The gambler kicked his chair back, still glaring at Kate Masters. The girl's face was pale, the color of putty. Her mouth moved but she was too frightened to make a sound. McCain had overlooked the possibility of second dealing completely. At this moment all his hate was directed at the girl who he thought had double-crossed him. That was a turn that I hadn't anticipated.

He said hoarsely, almost whispered, "I'll be seeing you, Kate!" and he wheeled and started for the door. Phil Carney stepped forward, directly in McCain's path.

"You've got another hand to play, McCain! That's the deal you made!"

The gambler didn't even see him; he was too angry to see or hear or even feel. Slim Kasper fell in beside him and the two of them went out into the startling brightness of the afternoon. I was just as glad that it was over.

Strangely enough, the kid didn't push his luck with McCain. He stood there for a moment, his face dark, then turned abruptly and grinned.

"You've done it, Jeff!"

All I wanted was sleep. Every inch of me ached for sleep as I stood up. I looked once at the frightened saloon girl, but I could feel no sympathy for her. She had deliberately switched that prepared deck on me. She had done that for McCain—after all the things he had done to her! Well, there was no understanding the workings of a woman's brain . . . or heart. But I wouldn't want to be in her shoes, the way McCain felt about her now.

I turned the bank over to Phil Carney and he stood there, staring at it, fondling it. "McCain's money!" he said softly, as though McCain's money were the only kind that was any good. "Do you know what this means, Jeff? He can't hold out on that ranch without money. He can't last until the Indian agents start buying again. This is almost as good as winning the ranch outright. It'll take a little longer, that's all."

That ranch! I was tired of it. I was sick of it and I was dead for sleep. I said, "Give the money to Stella. Have her lock it up in her safe. And let's get out of here."

The saloon crowd parted silently as we walked toward the door. They still didn't believe it. Their champion had fallen, they had seen it, but they still didn't quite believe it. We hit the plank walk and the dazzling sun was as shocking as a hammer blow. When had I slept last? When had I last relaxed and closed my eyes and thought of something besides cards? I couldn't remember.

I hoped the kid was right about that money. I hoped that he could somehow use it to pressure McCain off the ranch, but I wasn't going to think about it now. I wasn't even going to talk to Laura about it. I was just going to sleep.

And I did. I slept through the afternoon, through the night, and up to breakfasttime the next day. A long time. Too long, as it turned out, for while I was sleeping McCain had been working.

Chapter Eleven

It was before breakfast and I was outside at the washstand when I heard the horse pound up the street and wheel recklessly in front of the boardinghouse. There was always some fool cow hand acting up. When I started back up the stairs I heard the noise out on the front porch, but it didn't occur to me that anything was wrong until I got back to the room.

It was still dark and the coal-oil lamp on the dresser cast long, distorted shadows across the room. Phil Carney had just taken his revolver off a nail and was buckling the cartridge belt around his waist. It was the look on his face that jarred me.

I said, "You're going to be a little overdressed for breakfast, aren't you?"

His head jerked up. "You haven't heard?" he said tightly. "Stella Taggart's saloon was robbed last night!"

I missed the implication completely.

"Don't you understand?" he almost yelled. "They got into the saloon safe! They cleaned it out!"

My reaction was like getting shot with a particularly heavy bullet. At first there is nothing but shock and surprise, and then, slowly, you become aware of the fact that you are hurt.

All that money! That pouch of gold coins that the kid had given to me, as well as the money I had taken from McCain, all of it had been in the saloon safe! I'd had the kid put it there because, at the time, it seemed the smart thing to do. Stella Taggart's safe was a big hulking monster of a vault, as most saloon safes had to be. In cow towns they were almost like second banks, and it wasn't unusual for a cattleman or gambler to leave his money in one overnight for safekeeping.

I had trouble believing it. It didn't seem possible that such a situation could get even worse, but evidently it had. I said, "Does the Marshal know about this?"

"Everybody does! Silas Mills is gettin' a posse together. They're goin' out and beat the brush, but it won't do a damn bit of good. There's only one thing to do now."

"And that's what?" I thought I knew, but I asked anyway.

He was getting his hat now, ready to go. "I'm going to get McCain!"

"You're going to get yourself killed, you mean. Don't you think we'd better let the Marshal take care of things this time?"

He looked at me and snorted. "Silas Mills goes by the law, and the law works too slow to suit me."

He reached for the door and I said, "So you think McCain was in on the robbery?"

He laughed roughly. "What do *you* think?"

I thought that probably the kid was right.

Breakfast was on the table when we got downstairs, but there was no one there to eat it. All the boarders had disappeared in the direction of Stella's saloon to get a firsthand account of the robbery. Mrs. Lorring met us at the foot of the stairs, wringing her hands and complaining that the food was going to get cold. The kid, who could usually josh her into laughing, said nothing. Grim-faced, he walked straight for the front door and out of the house.

"Phil!" Laura was waiting for us on the front porch, and I guessed that she had already heard the story. "Phil, where are you going?"

He didn't even look at her. He tramped down the walk and swung into the street, heading toward town. "Jeff . . ." Laura was frightened now. I had seen her angry plenty of times, but this look of fear was something new. "Jeff, where is he going?"

"Where everybody else seems to be headed, I guess. Down to the saloon."

She knew I was lying, but she tried hard to believe it. "Jeff," she said tightly, "is it true, what they're saying? Is the money really gone?"

"It looks that way, but we can't be sure of anything until we talk to Silas Mills." I started walking toward the street when she stopped me again.

"Jeff, you've got to stop him. You can't let Phil go after—"

She let the words hang, but I knew what she meant. I was getting pretty tired of nursing a kid Phil Carney's age, but I said, "Don't worry. It'll come out all right." There was not much conviction in my voice.

There was quite a crowd in front of the saloon, and Marshal Silas Mills was bellowing like a mad bull. "Pat Lawson, you and Burt get down to the wagon yard and rustle up some horses. Be damn who the owners are, just get the horses down here. The rest of you, if you don't want to ride on this posse, then get out of the way, go on home." I pushed through the crowd and stepped up the plank walk where the Marshal was. "Well," he snarled, "what do *you* want?"

"What about this robbery?"

"A robbery's a robbery," he said impatiently. "What do you mean, what about it?"

"I had over two thousand in gold in Stella Taggart's safe. I want to know if it's gone."

The Marshal's face turned a slightly darker shade of red. "Why do you think these galoots bothered to rob the place? Of course it's gone!"

"They broke into that safe of Stella's?" I was still having trouble believing that anyone could open that safe without waking the whole town.

The Marshal snorted. "They didn't break into it, they just opened it. They came in sometime between midnight and sunup." Suddenly he wheeled and shouted angrily to a man in the crowd. "Goddamnit, Burt, I said get them horses down here!"

The Marshal began scattering the crowd and shouting more orders, and it was useless to try to get anything out of him. Phil Carney had disappeared somewhere. I went out into the street and he wasn't out there. I wanted to talk to Stella Taggart and find out what the Marshal had meant by saying the robbers had "opened" the safe, but I figured finding the kid was even more important right now. I elbowed my way down the plank walk and began jogging in the direction of the wagon yard.

When I got there Phil Carney was just swinging up on a wiry, mean-looking bay gelding. The corral gate was open and several men were trying to get loops around the skittish horses, and the kid didn't even see me in the confusion. I yelled to him and he looked at me blankly, that grimness set like cement at the corners of his mouth.

I said, "Wait till I get myself something to ride and we'll go back down to the saloon together. The Marshal's already organizing a search party."

Carney reined up in front of me. "No, thanks," he said tightly. "I don't have to ask the Marshal who broke into that saloon. And when I find McCain, I don't aim to be held back by any posse."

He touched the reins to the gelding's neck and the animal reared suddenly and almost came down on top of me. Then, before I could stop him or even yell at him, he was gone. That bay horse brushed past me and pounded up the street away from the gathering posse.

My first thoughts were: Let him go! Let the damn fool get himself killed, if that's what he wants! To hell with him!

But I thought of Laura. I had promised to keep

the kid from doing anything crazy, and I had already failed in that. If I let him get killed . . . I didn't want to think about that, so I grabbed a lariat from a corral post and went fishing for one of those livery horses.

It was almost like being in the van of a stampede, in that corral. The horses were excited and plunging and snorting, and the men were just as bad. The liveryman was yelling that they couldn't take those horses, but they were taking them anyway. What's more, they had kicked open the door to the saddle shed and were taking the saddles too. The liveryman yelled that he would call the Marshal. Then he brandished a big hog-leg .44 and swore he'd kill the next sonofabitch to touch hemp to one of his horses, but he didn't. I cut out a big red critter with a wild look in his eye and finally got him gentled enough to throw up a saddle and get it buckled down. I had to wrestle him for a while to get him to take the bit, but finally I got him rigged out and climbed aboard.

I was ready to go, but I didn't know where. The kid was already out of sight. Over by the gate there was a big hawk-nosed cow hand trying to get his saddle cinched down, and I rode over and shouted:

"How do I get to the McCain outfit?"

He looked up blankly, sweat pouring off his ugly face. "What?"

"The Carney place. How do I get to it?"

He seemed to be thinking: What kind of a damn-fool question is that? But he was obliging and gave me the directions, and while he was doing it his horse got away from him. "Goddamnit!" he yelled. "Come back here, you bald-faced, spavined, knock-kneed—" I nudged my own red horse through the gate and headed up the street without waiting to hear the rest of it.

According to the cow hand, the way to get to the old Carney ranch was to follow the wagon road east out of town until you came to a creek bed, which would probably be dry, and then you left the road and headed southeast until you reached a place called Hogback Ridge. The ranch was on the other side of that somewhere. I didn't know exactly where, and the cow hand had been too busy to say, but I guessed that I could find it without much trouble. If some of McCain's men didn't find me first.

As I rode away from the Marshal's posse, I remembered that grim look of determination that had been in Phil Carney's face, and I knew that he was heading straight for a shoot-out with the gambler. My insides twisted at the thought. It would be the same as suicide, going gunning for a man on his own property.

At that moment I didn't care a damn about that wild-eyed kid, but I did care about Laura, and that meant that I had to stop him. It wasn't going to be easy. The cow hand who had given me the directions hadn't mentioned that once you left the road you ran into a sea of waist-high brush and dagger thorns. And he hadn't mentioned the abrupt gullies and dry washes that leaped at you from every direction and out of nowhere. It was the first time I had ever ridden in such country. Luckily, that red livery horse knew more about brush travel than I did, and I soon learned to give him his head.

There was no sign of the kid at all. I couldn't see how a man could beat his way through this brush and not leave some kind of trail—but then, Phil Carney knew this country and probably hadn't turned off the road the same place I had. By the time I reached the place called Hogback Ridge, the slow, heavy hand of anxiety began to bear down on me. Although by this time the sun was blazing hot, the chill of uneasiness began to take hold of me.

Still no sign.

I had figured it would be comparatively easy to catch up with him, but he had got away clean. That same savage country stretched out before me, the monotony of brushland broken here and there by small knolls and gullies. There was not a tree in sight more than shoulder-high. Certainly it was no place for hiding. But where had he gone?

I got my answer in the form of a small, round sound, almost lost in that great vastness of space and brush. It was the sound of a rifle, very far away.

I came up in the saddle as the implication of that small sound hit me. Then I slammed that red horse in the ribs and we ripped through the thicket of scrubby blackjack until we had gained the crest of the ridge.

In the far distance I could see the chimney of a house and the steep slanting roofs of two barns, and I guessed that I was looking at the headquarters buildings of what had once been the Carney ranch. The country around it seemed to be as wild as the rest of this part of Texas, and I remember wondering, in the back of my mind, How could a man possibly run a paying ranch in this kind of country? How do the cattle find enough to eat?

I had no idea how they did it, but apparently they managed. Below me, next to a gully, a scattering of saber-horned steers muzzled in the brownish, dead-looking grass that seemed to cover the ground like a carpet. Off to the south more cattle dotted the landscape—but I wasn't interested in cattle right then. As I stared, four horsemen seemed to appear from nowhere, until I realized that they must have come out of one of those gullies. They were still several hundred yards away, but not so far that I couldn't recognize two of them.

One was Jay McCain and one was his side man, Slim Kasper. The other two I had never seen before, but I guessed that they must be part of

McCain's crew. They rode easily, completely relaxed. I seemed to freeze for a moment as I watched them. One of them had fired that rifle. Just one shot.

Evidently they had been satisfied that one shot had been enough. There was no sign of the kid anywhere.

Then, as some terrible fascination held me motionless, a horse leaped out of one of the dry washes like a startled swamp rabbit, crashed through the brush at a dead run, and disappeared behind one of the knolls. I had seen that horse before. It was the bay gelding that Phil Carney had ridden out of the wagon yard back at Sabina.

But the saddle was empty.

I don't know how long I would have stayed there, held immobile with numbness, if McCain and his men hadn't seen me. But they did see me. I heard one of them shout, then they wheeled their mounts to face the ridge, and the next thing I knew another rifle had split the desert morning wide open.

If I had been smart, I would have put iron to red horse and got out of there. But that wasn't my day to be smart. In my mind I could see Phil Carney down there somewhere in the brush, crumpled and very small in death. I didn't remember, at that moment, all the trouble that kid had brought me to. I didn't remember his lying and scheming. I remembered him as a man who had fought with

172

amazing valor with Hood's Texans, as a man who had saved my own life more than once.

My anger was suddenly alive and full grown and burning, an anger too hot and too big for one brain to hold.

It is possible that too much anger drove me slightly crazy for a few minutes. Four rifles were barking at me now, but the agonizing sound of bullets burning the thin air held no meaning for me. Recklessly I drove my red horse down the steep slope of the ridge, noticing neither gullies nor brush. I had a single purpose at that moment, one reason in life, and that was to kill the man who had killed Phil Carney. And I knew that man was Jay McCain.

How they missed me and that red horse, I can't say. Probably they weren't used to idiots riding hell for leather right down the barrels of their rifles, and the sight of such a thing had rattled them. Anyway, they were jerking off their shots and missing, and that was the important thing. What I expected to do, I don't know. I wasn't thinking that far ahead. All I wanted at that moment was to get my hands on McCain's bull-like neck and slowly, with immense pleasure, squeeze the life out of him. It never occurred to me that those other three riflemen might have other ideas.

I had almost reached the bottom of the slope when my unbelievable string of luck played out.

That big red was a good, sure-footed, almost bottomless animal, but he wasn't good enough for the way I was pushing him. Maybe it was a break in the land, or maybe it was just a hole or a rock. It happened too fast to find out. That red horse went down. He crashed down on the back of his neck as though he had been poleaxed. I left the saddle and crashed to the ground with a bone-shattering jar and the breath went out of me.

I could see McCain and the others coming toward me and I couldn't move, couldn't even bring myself to my knees. They had their rifles ready, and I thought: I'd just as soon miss these next few seconds. I had been shot once in the war, and it was nothing to look forward to.

Then, as I was thinking what a lousy place this was to die in, the four of them stopped. As if I were watching something in a dream, I saw their heads snap up, a look of startled bewilderment on their faces. The sound came an instant later. One, two, three big mushy explosions of a revolver.

It wasn't the ear-splitting crack that a high-velocity rifle makes at close range, so it had to be a revolver. But none of the four men had reached for his holster. Dazedly I wondered about that. Then I thought: By God, Denfield, this is a chance you'll never get again, and you'd better take it!

I took it. While McCain and his men were still being surprised by the new attack, I managed to push myself up and run. Where I was going I didn't know; I just knew that I had to run. That red horse started to run too, but I didn't know until later that he had almost run the bushwhackers down. Behind me, McCain and his men were scattering like chickens in front of a runaway Concord as the frightened animal blasted through them and headed toward Mexico. But all I knew was that they weren't shooting at me right then, and that was enough to make me happy for a while.

That fall had almost torn the shirt off my back, and my arm was bleeding but didn't seem to be broken, and if it had been broken it wouldn't have made much difference because I was interested in running right then and nothing else. I kept searching for some place to make a stand, but there didn't seem to be any place unless it would be behind some scraggly blackjack, and they didn't look very substantial. I heard somebody yelling, but I figured it was McCain, and anyway I was too busy running to pay attention.

By this time I had spotted a gully up ahead. It was the prettiest gully I had ever seen, a deep, wide, raw gash in the ground that a man could crawl into and maybe get a chance to fight back for a change. It was about fifty yards in front of me, and every step of the way I expected McCain's crew to start burning me down, but they didn't. Of course, I didn't know about the horse then, and I had almost forgotten about the unknown pistoleer that had handed me my break in the first place.

The important thing was to get to that gully. If I was lucky I would make it to that dry wash; then I could settle back and consider all the mistakes I had made before those four riflemen closed in and wrote finish to everything. That was when I saw Phil Carney.

I shouldn't have been surprised, considering all I had been through with him, but the Carney bag of tricks was bottomless and they never failed to jar me. He was on a small knoll, beyond the gully I was heading for. Standing beside a house-sized boulder, he was waving both arms and yelling at me.

About three steps from the gully I began laughing. There was absolutely nothing funny in the situation, but a touch of hysteria took hold of me and I felt that if I didn't laugh I would do something much worse. I hit the dry wash on my belly and lay there laughing for a full five seconds—and, just as suddenly as it had started, the laughter was gone.

"Jeff, up here!" Phil Carney was yelling.

To hell with you! I thought. Goddamn you and to hell with you!

"Get out of that gully, man! You can still make it!"

Then I saw what he meant. At the lower end of the draw I heard the jingle of spurs as someone slipped down the embankment. Then I heard

McCain shouting for somebody to get at the other end and the picture began to come to me. All they had to do was close in on me from both ends and let one of the boys shoot me when they smoked me out. That gully that had looked so nice and safe a few minutes before was now a death trap.

Chapter Twelve

All the cover Phil Carney could give me was with a revolver. That was pretty ineffective, but it would have to do. I vaulted over the far bank of the gully and began running, and this time my luck stuck with me. I made it behind the knoll just as the rifles were beginning to get my range.

The kid was on one knee behind that big boulder, methodically taking pot shots at whatever he could see, which couldn't have been much, because McCain and his boys were out of sight now. Down in the gully, probably, holding a council of war.

"It's lucky you got out of that wash," Phil Carney called down to me.

"Thanks for giving me a hand," I said bitterly. "I don't know what I'd do without you."

The half grin he had been wearing began to slip. "We'd better get somethin' straight," he said evenly. "I didn't ask you to this party, Jeff."

"But I came just the same."

"Laura?" he asked.

"It happens that your sister doesn't want to see you killed. Is there something wrong in that?"

He laughed shortly and without humor, then turned his attention back to the gully. I made my way up to that big rock and checked my revolver and gave my breathing a chance to get back to normal.

"What happened?" I said finally. "Has McCain turned to bushwhacking?"

He made that sound again that was supposed to be laughter. "He and Kasper and the two riders were waiting for me in that arroyo over there. One of them burned a bullet across the gelding's withers and the horse threw me. I guess they thought I was dead."

"If there was any justice," I said, "you would be. Who ever told you you could outsmart a man like McCain, much less outshoot him?"

He didn't even look at me. "I told you you wasn't invited to this party. If you don't like it, you can leave now."

"You know what's going to happen, don't you?" I asked dryly. "If a miracle should happen and you managed somehow to kill McCain, the courts would call it murder because you're trespassing on his property. If he kills you, the courts will call it self-defense for the same reason."

"What am I supposed to do?" he asked tightly. "McCain stole every penny I had, he stole my chance of getting back my ranch. Am I supposed to just take it?"

"You might let the Marshal play his hand out and see for sure who stole the money." A short laugh was Phil Carney's only comment to that. "You've decided to take the law in your own hands," I went on. "I've got a hunch Silas Mills isn't going to like that."

"To hell with Silas Mills." Then he turned on me, that faint grin touching the corners of his mouth again. "How would *you* like it to go?" he asked. "Would you like me to just sit back and let the Marshal flounder around until the excitement wore off and people forgot there had even been a robbery? Would you like to see Laura marry Jay McCain?" His grin grew a bit more bitter. "She'd do it, you know. In spite of you or me or anybody else, she'll get that ranch back one way or another."

I said nothing.

"You know she would, don't you, Jeff?"

"There won't be much point in it if we don't get off this knoll pretty soon."

Then, as we watched the gully for some sign of movement, I began wondering about something else. As I thought back on it, this whole business of bushwhacking didn't make a great amount of sense. It didn't stand to reason that McCain would deliberately set out to murder Phil Carney, unless he had completely given up the idea of getting

Laura—and that I seriously doubted. Of course, if it ever came to a do-or-die shoot-out between Carney and the gambler, McCain would have no choice, but that wasn't the way it had happened.

"They're takin' a hell of a long time tryin' to make up their minds to charge this rock," the kid said, almost to himself.

I was thinking the same thing. I tried to put myself in McCain's shoes, and asked myself what I would do if I had three men down there in the gully and he was up here on the knoll. The answer was simple. I would cover that rock from the four points of the compass, and before long the battle would be over.

So why didn't the gambler do it? Certainly he was as smart as the next man, and he must have figured it out for himself by now.

I looked at Phil Carney. He was still on one knee, the revolver in his hand and his face completely impassive, showing no trace of fear. I had seen him like that before. Behind the breastworks at Bloody Angle. Waiting for one of the endless Yankee charges at The Wilderness. He still wore that floppy, battered Confederate campaign hat, almost an exact drab replica of the one I was wearing myself. I could almost imagine that it was the war all over again. Once again I could almost hear the sodden tramping of soldiers. . . .

Abruptly my mind snapped back to the present. I was staring again at Phil Carney and that old campaign hat that he wore. I thought I knew why McCain was taking so long to make his decision.

The only way to explain it was that the bushwhack try at the kid had been a mistake. He probably hadn't even expected the kid to come after him, but he had sure been waiting for somebody, and that somebody was me! It began to make sense now. *I* was the one he wanted to get rid of, not Phil Carney. The kid and I were pretty close to the same size, we both wore those floppy campaign hats. They weren't very fashionable, maybe, but they were distinctive. I didn't have to stretch my imagination to see how McCain could have mistaken the kid for me, especially at the distance he had been shooting from.

Well, by God! I thought. I was beginning to get mad all over again. My luck was going to change one of these days and McCain was going to make good with one of his tries at fitting me to a coffin. I had been shot at before, but this was the first time I'd ever had someone deliberately set out to murder me. I had to come to Sabina for that!

Oh, Sabina was quite a place, all right! A man could learn a lot of things here, if he could somehow manage to stay alive. I hated this scraggly, monotonous, tiger-wild piece of landscape more than I had ever hated a place before—but about the last thing I planned to do right now was leave. I had a little piece of business to settle with a man named McCain. . . .

I realized then that Phil Carney was speaking. "It looks like they've finally decided."

I saw them. They came out of the gully and darted into the brush before we could do anything with our revolvers. I said, "Pretty soon this fortress of yours isn't going to be much better than the wash." But he wasn't listening. Phil Carney was beginning to get the picture now and he wasn't liking it. Those riflemen could keep out of revolver range and still be plenty close to pick us off that knoll when they got into position.

I still didn't think that McCain would go for the kid. What he had finally decided, I figured, was that they would just sit back and do a little sharpshooting at some vital part of my anatomy, and after that was over they could ride away and let the kid do what he pleased. But I didn't express my ideas to Phil Carney. Let him sweat, goddamn him.

About that time a lead bullet smashed into the boulder about a foot over my head, and right behind it came the smart, businesslike crack of a rifle, and I knew the battle had started. I hit the ground, with the kid right in front of me, and we squirmed around to the other side of the boulder, but that wasn't much better. Phil Carney was cursing quietly and bitterly.

"If we just had some rifles!"

Some horses would come in handy, too, I thought. But that big red of mine had probably

182

crossed the Mexican border by this time. The kid was on his belly up ahead of me, his position even more exposed than mine. But the rifle fire was all coming my way, which was no surprise now. One slug gouged the ground at my side and went screaming off into the endless blue of the desert morning. They were getting my range, and there was nothing I could do about it. I burned three cartridges, but the distance was much too great for a revolver.

Shooting back did no good, but the feel of a bucking gun in my hand made me feel a little better, so I let go again and began reloading. I tried to push back that damp cold feeling of futility. I tried to convince myself that it was still a fight and we would get out of it somehow.

But I knew better. It was just a matter of time. Sooner or later one of those bullets was going to find its mark, and that would be the end of Jeff Denfield. The law of averages is one law you can't break. Then, even as I thought it, as I rammed the last cartridge in the cylinder, McCain's men stopped the battle.

It didn't make sense. They had me exactly where they wanted me. It wasn't like McCain to knock off in the middle of a job like that. I looked at Phil Carney and he looked back at me, and neither of us could figure it out until we heard the sound in the distance.

Horses. A big bunch of them. Ten, maybe

fifteen, but I couldn't see a thing. Then the kid made a startled sound and motioned behind me, and when I looked around they had just topped the crest of Hogback Ridge and were coming toward us, Marshal Silas Mills in the van.

I looked at my hands and found that they were shaking. I didn't know what the Marshal was doing here, but I was glad he had decided to make the trip. For a few minutes there I could almost see that coffin that McCain had been measuring for me. It doesn't do a man's nerves any good to go through an experience like that.

Silas Mills's methods were very businesslike and effective. If McCain had had any ideas about leaving the scene, he was forced to revise them. The Marshal had already sent four men to round up the gambler and his fellow bushwhackers, and now Mills himself was heading toward the knoll. He didn't say a word, but dismounted at the bottom of the slope and waited for us to come down. Only when we reached level ground again did I see rage in the big man's eyes.

But Phil Carney didn't see it. "Well, Marshal," he said grimly, "the trail led to McCain after all, didn't it? Just the way I told you it would."

The possemen had rounded up McCain's boys and were bringing them toward the knoll, but I had lost interest in them now. At that moment the Marshal turned on Phil Carney, his small eyes blazing. "Thanks to you, Carney," he said roughly, "there's no trail to follow. And if there is one, it's too cold now to do us any good." He spat at the ground, glancing first at me, then at the kid.

Phil Carney stared blankly, trying to digest what the Marshal had fed him. "Do you mean," he asked tightly, "that you didn't even try to pick up the robbers' trail? What kind of a lawman are you?"

With no word of warning, the Marshal reached out an enormous hand and grabbed the front of Phil Carney's shirt, almost jerking the kid's feet off the ground. "There's somethin' you better get straight, son," he said with deadly calm. "I'm the law here in Sabina. Nobody can tell me how to run my business, not even a Carney."

The Marshal's sudden action had stunned the kid into silence, for a moment anyway. He dangled, almost comically, from the end of Mills's big fist. Most of the possemen had gathered around now, and they shuffled uncomfortably at this strange sight of a Carney being put in his place. "Listen to me," the Marshal said. "And, goddamn you, you'd better listen good. When I figure a man needs killin' in Sabina County, I'll do it myself. I don't want any help from smart-aleck kids. Is that clear?"

I knew it wasn't going to last. No one, not even Mills, could completely subdue that Carney temper. The kid seemed to recognize the ridiculous situation he was in. "Goddamn you, Silas!" he yelled. "Turn loose of me!" But the big lawman had no intention of letting go. Carney lashed out at the Marshal's face, but Mills merely tightened his grip and twisted the kid away. Then, methodically, effortlessly, Silas Mills began shaking him. He did it as easily as a terrier would shake a rat. I could hear Phil Carney's teeth rattling. He dangled and squirmed at the end of the Marshal's big fist like a badly made scarecrow spinning in a high wind.

"Don't you goddamn me, son!" the Marshal said in cold anger. Then he turned loose of the kid and cracked him solidly across the face with the back of his fist. The kid dropped like a brain-shot steer, and Silas Mills stood towering over him, glowering down at him. "Don't you ever goddamn me again," he repeated.

I had moved in instinctively. Why I felt that I was obligated to take Phil Carney's part, I don't know; maybe by now it was getting to be a matter of habit. I had taken only one step when a half-dozen saddle guns turned in my direction.

The Marshal had put Phil Carney from his mind. The kid could have been a spider that Mills had stepped on, kicked away, and forgotten about. He gave me no more than a glance, as though to say I wasn't worth bothering with. Spread-legged, mad at the world, he stood there, and after a moment he barked, "Bishop, you and Matt take this kid away before I do something I'll be sorry for later on."

For the moment the fight had been knocked out of Phil Carney. The possemen pulled him to his feet and led him away. There was an ugly bruise across his left cheek and his nose was dripping blood down the front of his shirt. There was nothing I could do, so I decided to be quiet and see what Mills was going to do with McCain.

I was surprised to see that the gambler looked completely unworried as Mills's boys brought him and the others in. Back-shooting, I had supposed, was a serious offense, even in Sabina. But it didn't seem to bother McCain. He even smiled a little as he said:

"What's the meaning of this, Marshal? This Yankee and that crazy Carney kid are the ones you want, not me."

The word "Yankee" raised the hackles on my neck. After sitting the war out in Sabina, he still had the gall . . .

But this was the Marshal's party, and he was going to run it exactly the way he wanted it run. All I could do now was add it to the growing list of debts and hope that I'd get the chance to pay them off someday, in full. "All right," Silas was saying wearily, as though he were sick of this mess and eager to get out of it. "What's your story, McCain?"

"It's perfectly clear," the gambler said evenly, almost pleasantly. "That crazy kid got the idea that I had somethin' to do with robbin' Stella

Taggart's saloon last night. Me and the boys here were out gatherin' strays when he jumped us. Came out of the wash back there and tried to dry-gulch us."

"That's a goddamn lie!" the kid yelled, but the two possemen silenced him in a hurry. I couldn't tell if the Sabina citizens were beginning to lose their awe of the Carney name or if they were just afraid of Silas Mills. I had a feeling that it was a little of both. The Marshal didn't even bother to look around; he kept staring at McCain.

He said, "How did you know Stella's place was robbed last night?"

The gambler pointed to one of his sidemen. "Frank here was in town, just got back a while ago. Just a few minutes before that kid jumped us."

I couldn't figure that marshal out. He hated Jay McCain plenty—you had only to look at his eyes to know that—but it seemed to me that he was leaning over backward to make it easy for the gambler. He turned now and pointed toward the ridge. "Is that your boundary line?"

"Sure," McCain said. "That damn kid came onto my own land and tried to kill me. Look here, Marshal, I want something—"

"You'll get something," Mills broke in coldly. "The same thing Carney got, if you try to tell me how to run my business."

That cooled McCain off. He didn't like being talked to like that, but he wasn't going to make an issue of it. He shrugged. "All right, figure it out for yourself. I've got three witnesses here to back up my story."

Then I said, "Marshal, don't you think you'd better listen to the kid's side of it, too?"

He turned on me as though I had pulled a knife on him. "That's enough out of you, Denfield. What I have to say to you will keep until we get back to town."

I couldn't figure it out. I couldn't get mad at a man who had just saved my life, but I sure couldn't see any sense in the way he was handling this. Some of the posse members were pretty puzzled about it, too. Here the Marshal had got them together for the purpose of tracking down some robbers, and the first thing they knew, they'd wound up right in the middle of somebody's private feud.

I began to get the feeling that they somehow blamed the whole thing on me. The Marshal was a man they had understood and respected for a long time. It was perfectly clear that they still respected him and his judgment, but they were beginning to wonder if they really understood him as well as they thought they had. That made them uncomfortable, and vaguely angry, and when they began to look around for somebody to pin their anger onto, there I was.

I wondered what they used for a whipping boy before Jeff Denfield came to town.

The Marshal was saying, "If you want to file charges, McCain, you'll have to come into town and make out a complaint."

"I don't want to file charges," the gambler said, almost smiling as he glanced at me. "I just want that crazy kid kept off my property."

Did *McCain* want to file charges! A man engineers a neat, cold-blooded little scheme to murder you, and they ask him if he wants to file charges!

"Look . . ." I started to say, but the Marshal was on me before I could get the thought into words.

"I'll talk to you when we get to town, Denfield! Two of you men will have to ride double," he said to his men. "Denfield and Carney will take the extra horse. We're goin' back to Sabina."

I stood there with my mouth open, not entirely believing that it could be brought to an end like that, with no fuss at all. Not even a question about the stolen money. But it seemed that the Marshal could end it any way he pleased, and this was the way he wanted it.

"By God, Marshal," I said, "I've got a piece to say and I want to say it!"

I knew what the answer was going to be even before he turned to me. "When we get to town, Denfield. Don't make me tell you again!"

My patience was about to snap. I said, "God-damnit, I'm going to talk whether you want to hear it or not!"

But I was wrong. I saw the big lawman nod, but I didn't get the meaning until it was too late. Much too late. By that time the posseman behind me had already started swinging.

Chapter Thirteen

I was in the saddle and Phil Carney was riding behind, trying to hold me erect.

"How do you feel?" he asked.

"How am I supposed to feel? Who hit me, anyway?"

"One of Mills's men caught you with a pistol butt. By God, I thought you were dead, the way you dropped!"

I wasn't dead yet, but I had the feeling that it was a temporary arrangement. There was an egg-sized bump over my left ear. I felt of it. It was like pushing a button on a switch-blade knife. The pain went all the way to my groin.

For several minutes I was too sick to talk. I concentrated on not falling out of the saddle, wondering what Silas Mills had planned for us when he got us back to Sabina. Well, anyway, I thought, I'd managed to get out of it without getting killed, and maybe that was something.

We got back on the wagon road finally and that blowtorch sun was right on top of us. The kid hadn't said a word for several minutes, and after a while his stiff silence began to get on my nerves. When Phil Carney was silent for more than a minute it was a pretty sure bet that he was cooking up another crazy scheme in that brain of his.

"Just forget it," I said.

"Forget what?"

"Whatever you're thinking about. We've had enough trouble for one day."

When he spoke again he didn't sound angry, only thoughtful. And that surprised me. "Jeff," he said, "there's something crazy here. Do you think Silas Mills could have thrown in with McCain on that robbery?"

"What makes you ask a question like that? I had the idea that the Marshal hated McCain's guts."

I could feel him shrug. "Maybe . . ." And I knew that temper of his was coming to the top again. "But Silas sure as hell didn't put himself out trying to trail the robbers. And the Marshal knows as well as anybody that McCain is the sonofabitch that took that money." We rode for perhaps two full minutes before he went on. "But I just can't believe it about Silas Mills," he said. "He was one of my father's best friends. He's lived in Sabina all his life and been marshal as long as I can remember. No. I just can't believe that he'd throw in with a man like McCain."

As we neared town, I decided that the kid was right. I didn't especially like the way Mills was running the show, but I still couldn't see him taking his orders from a crooked gambler. Or anybody else, for that matter. Maybe, I thought, the Marshal knows what he's doing. After all, he's been at the business for a long time, and maybe he knows a lot of things that we don't. It was just possible that McCain had nothing to do with the robbery. Or maybe Silas was playing a game of nerves, hoping that McCain would hang himself if he got enough rope.

I didn't know. There was a thundering ache inside my head and it didn't seem worth the trouble trying to figure it out. But there was one thing I wanted to be sure of.

I turned to the kid. "We'll be coming into town pretty soon. Maybe Silas will tell us what's on his mind, but whether he does or not, I want you to promise to sit tight until we get a chance to talk it out."

He looked away, his mouth pulled tight.

"Goddamnit," I said, "I don't intend to walk into another murder trap because of some damn-fool stunt of yours. I'll get that promise or you'll get one from me. I'll catch the next stage out of this God-forgotten place!"

Actually, I don't think I could have done it. I was in too deep. I had too many scores to settle to bow out now, like an old Southern gentleman politely excusing himself from a tea party. And besides, there was Laura. So I don't think I'd really have caught that stage, but I was mad enough at that moment to make the kid think I would. I said, "Do I get a promise that you'll behave yourself?"

"All right." Grudgingly.

We'd hit Sabina's Main Street by now. Most of the town had turned out to see what the Marshal's posse had caught, and it occurred to me that Silas Mills must be feeling pretty silly about now. The townspeople seemed puzzled as they began gathering around, shouting questions at the sheepish posse members. Silas, I thought, I hope your reputation as a lawman is plenty solid. You're going to need something solid after a fiasco like this!

Stella Taggart was waiting for us in front of the saloon, and standing with her were Kate Masters and a few customers who had come out to see what the excitement was about. Stella shouted at the Marshal, but he only touched his hat and said, "After a while, Stella. I've got somethin' to do first." Then he reined up in the middle of the street. "All right, boys, you might as well go home. There's nothin' else we can do right now."

The posse that had started out so full of vinegar a few hours ago was now merely a group of sheepish cow hands and shopkeepers who were concentrating on being as inconspicuous as possible. Mills turned to me. "Denfield, I want to talk to you over at the office."

"What about me?" Phil Carney said. "I've got somethin' to say in this matter, too."

The Marshal gave him that flat look of his. "Carney," he said evenly, "you go home and tell your sister to look after you. You don't seem old enough to do it yourself."

For a moment I thought the kid was going to blow up, promise or no promise. He came ramrod erect in the saddle as color rushed to his face. But some inner caution must have warned him. Without a word, he jerked the horse around and headed up the street toward the corral.

I waited while the Marshal tied his horse at the rack in front of the saloon, then followed him up the street and back to the shack that he called an office. I was surprised to see that Kate Masters, the saloon girl, was there waiting for us. She was even more surprised at seeing me.

"What is it, Kate?" the Marshal said. He could speak softly, even gently, when he wanted to. And he spoke that way now.

The girl looked at me, then away. She was quite a woman, all right. It would take me a long while to forget that cold deck that she had switched in on me. A girl like that might have the answers to a lot of things, and answers were something I needed—but I had a feeling that this wasn't the time to bring it up. She said to the Marshal, "Stella wants to see you, when you get time."

She was a frightened girl as she backed toward

the door, and I didn't blame her. It was going to take a lot of explaining to convince McCain that she hadn't framed him.

The Marshal eased himself into a leather-bottomed chair behind his plank desk and motioned me toward a chair near the door. "Well, Denfield," he said, and the roughness was back in his voice, "you've given us about enough trouble here in Sabina, you and that Carney kid."

"*I've* given you trouble!" Anger hit me and I practically yelled it at him. "Look here, Marshal, has it ever occurred to you that McCain might have had a part in it, that he might have had something to do with what trouble you've had? Do you realize that he tried to kill Phil Carney this morning? He had mistaken Carney for me, most likely, but that wouldn't have made the kid any less dead if the bullet had come a few inches closer."

His thoughts seemed turned inward as he looked at me. "The Carney boy," he said quietly, "was trespassing on McCain's property. And so were you, for that matter."

"Is trespassing an offense to be shot for?" I demanded furiously.

He nodded, unsmiling. "It has been. You had no right to be on his land."

I kept telling myself to hold my anger in check, but it wasn't easy. "Look," I said. "Don't you think we'd better get back to the original problem and stop worrying so much about trespassing on

McCain's property? Sometime last night Stella's place was robbed, and whoever did it got away with every dollar the Carneys had. Don't you think it's about time to do something about that?"

He was thinking of something else and almost smiled. "Do you have anything to suggest?" he asked absently.

"I sure as hell have. I suggest that you pin McCain down and make him prove to you that he wasn't in town last night or early this morning, when Stella's safe was broken into."

"The safe wasn't broken into," he said. "It was opened. Somebody who knew the combination just came in and opened it. And I'm tired of hearing about McCain. He's not the only man in the world who would stoop to steal two thousand in gold." Then he did smile. "Even *Carney* gold."

That stopped me for a minute. I finally said, "Could McCain have known the combination?"

"Sure," he said, and reached for a corncob pipe that lay on the desk. "I guess so, anyway. But so could a hundred other people. Plenty of people have seen Stella open that safe. If a man was standin' in just the right place and payin' attention, there's no reason why he couldn't catch on to the combination by watching her do it."

I didn't believe it. That safe was too far away from the bar, and even if a man had the eyes of a hawk, he couldn't have learned anything from the other side of the bar. As I thought about it, the

Marshal calmly filled his pipe from a twist of tobacco, then lit it with a sulphur match.

I said, "If I were you, I'd still question McCain."

His fist came down on the desk with a crash that jarred the room. "I told you I'd heard enough about McCain!"

I made a mistake then. I said, "Are you afraid of McCain, Marshal? Is that the reason you don't want to mix with him?"

He came half out of his chair, eyes blazing. "You think you're pretty goddamn smart, don't you, Denfield? If you think you're smart enough to tell me how to run my business, you've got another think comin'!"

"It seems like *somebody* ought to tell you, Marshal. You're sure not doing much good the way you're going." It wasn't a smart thing to say, but I was mad and didn't care at the moment whether Mills liked it or not.

He leaned over the desk, his voice suddenly very cold and calm. "All right, Denfield, you asked for it. I was goin' to try to go easy on you, but you won't have it that way, will you? Your kind always has to make a show of being smart." Suddenly he spat at the floor. "If I see that face of yours after ten o'clock tomorrow morning, I'll lock you up. I'll lock you up every time I see you, and don't tell me that I have to have a reason. I'm marshal of Sabina, and that's reason enough for folks down here!"

I came to my feet at that, not angry now, but frankly stunned. "Are you threatening me, Marshal?"

"I'm just tellin' you I don't want to see you after ten o'clock tomorrow mornin'."

"Why ten o'clock?"

"That's when the next stage pulls out of Sabina. And, by God, you'd better be on it, if you know what's good for you!"

It didn't strike me as being very funny, but I could feel the nervous laughter starting somewhere in my bowels, and when it worked its way up to my throat I couldn't stop it. I threw my head back and howled. I half expected him to lean across the desk and hit me full in the face, but I guess that laughter surprised him as much as it did me.

"So you think it's funny, do you?" he shouted. "Well, by God, I meant every word of it! You'd better be on that stage!"

"This is the damnedest thing I ever heard!" I managed to say. "It seems like half the people in Sabina spend most of their time trying to get me on a stage!"

"I'm not 'most people,' Denfield. I'm the law in Sabina and I'm sick of lookin' at you!"

"You mean you're afraid I'll find out why you won't face up to McCain, don't you, Marshal?"

There was a funny look in his eyes. He said, "Denfield, there's been nothin' but trouble in this town since the day you hit here. We've had all the trouble we want, and that's why you're leavin', understand?" Then, with absolutely no change in expression, he hit me.

The minute we had stepped inside the office I think I knew that it would end like this. The Marshal was spoiling for a fight. I didn't know just what was bothering him, and I didn't particularly care right then. Although I was no match for Silas Mills, I still welcomed any outlet for the tremendous amount of steam that my anger had built up inside me. All right, I thought, as I saw that big fist coming at me. They may have to carry me out in pieces, but you're going to know you've been in a fight, Marshal!

I was wrong again. That fist exploded like a bomb just below the angle of my jaw and I went to my knees. I tried to get up but something had happened to my coordination. My arms and legs simply wouldn't do what my brain told them. I had never been hit that hard before, and still I had the frightening feeling that Silas hadn't even tried to hurt me. It was just his way of brushing his enemies aside. He looked at me coldly for one long moment, then jammed his hat on his head and tramped out of the office.

I must have stayed on the floor for a full two minutes before my confused brain finally got the order straight and my leg muscles began to react. I made it to the leather-bottomed chair and dropped there for another few minutes. It seems you never know about these people, I thought bitterly. You think a man is on your side and suddenly he turns on you like a tiger.

While I sat there I knew that I had a decision to make. The most important decision I'd ever had put to me. And once I'd made it, there would be no backing out.

But it was one of those decisions that was practically ready-made. I had never been run out of a town before, and pure bullheadedness refused to let me begin now. I would be damned if I would!

I was still sitting there, holding my anger down while I played along the outer edges of a new idea. To start with, I was now convinced that McCain had taken that money. How else could he have guessed that I might be coming after him on this particular day? He had taken it, all right; he was much too satisfied with himself for it to be otherwise. He had me just where he wanted me. With one bold stroke he had wiped me out. I sat back and thought about it, almost glad that it had happened this way. That crazy poker scheme of the kid's would never have worked anyway, but the sparring was over now. We could now get down to the deadly process of elimination, and the last man left standing would be the winner.

Well, McCain, you claim to be a gambler. This is where we start gambling for keeps.

Outside, I heard the tramp of boots and I knew it was Phil Carney even before he stepped inside the office and said:

"I just saw Mills go into Stella's saloon. What did he want to talk to you about?"

I looked up. "The Marshal thinks I'm a disturbing influence in this quiet little village of yours. He just invited me to get out of town—or else."

The kid was surprised. "Mills ordered you out of Sabina? What did he say about McCain?"

For no reason at all I felt myself grinning. "The Marshal doesn't like to talk about McCain. Can you think of any reason why Mills would be afraid to go up against McCain?"

"The Marshal? He's got a reputation for not being afraid of anything or anybody." He looked thoughtful. "You're right, though. It looks like McCain is holding a club of some kind over Mills's head. Have you got any idea what it is?"

My knees were still a little weak, but I stood up. "I want to think, and the only place to do it is in the Charleston House." He watched me as I walked out, then followed me around to the street. We had reached the feed store next to the saloon when I saw Kate Masters coming out of Stella's place. "Wait a minute," I said. "I want to talk to Kate."

"Talkin' to a girl like that on the street won't help your name in a town like this."

I hadn't realized before that Phil Carney was a snob, on top of a lot of other things. I said, "It might not help my name, but I don't figure it can hurt it much, either." Then I realized that he had probably been thinking about his sister. "All right," I said, "you go on to the Charleston House and I'll be along directly."

When Kate Masters saw me there was that strange look of surprise in her eyes hidden behind the glazed fear. She was in a tough spot. She had tried to cheat me, and McCain thought she had tried to cheat him, and she didn't know whom to be afraid of the most. I caught her arm just as she was about to turn back into the saloon. "Wait a minute, Kate. I want to talk to you."

"I . . . I can't now. I've got somethin' to do." The surprise was gone now. Only fear was left in those eyes of hers. She tried to jerk her arm free. "Let me go!"

"Look," I said. "You're going to need a friend when McCain comes back to town. Maybe I can help you. I'll try, anyway, if you'll tell me what you know about the robbery."

She laughed bitterly, but the sound stopped abruptly as she stared over my right shoulder. I could feel her shaking. "All right!" It was just a whisper; her lips hardly moved. "But in my shack, after the saloon closes!"

She was gone almost immediately, back into the saloon, and only then did I turn to see what she had been staring at. It was Slim Kasper, McCain's shadow. He was tying his horse at the rack in front of the general store, smiling that thin smile of his when he saw me watching him. Every time I saw him, every time I thought of him, I remembered that pistol whipping in the alley that night. Don't wait around to see me off on that stage tomorrow, I thought. I've got a personal score to settle with you, Kasper!

Still smiling, he hitched his revolver and went into the general store.

Chapter Fourteen

There was a frost-white moon out that night and a million stars shone bright and clean in the darkness over Sabina. It was after midnight, very late by Sabina standards, and the streets of the town were deserted except for two lonesome horses at the rack in front of Stella's saloon. I waited at the lower end of the street until I saw the lamps go out in front of the saloon. It was closing time and the last few stragglers came out and stood on the plank walk talking, looking up at the endless night. Visiting cow hands, probably.

I took a side street and came up behind the row of business buildings, all quiet now. After a while a back door opened and I saw Kate Masters come out of the saloon. I walked toward her and said:

"I've been waiting for you."

She made a startled sound, her face as white and cold as the moon. Then she saw me and sagged with relief. "Oh, it's you."

"Were you expecting McCain, or maybe Kasper?"

She backed away, as though she were afraid of getting too close to me. "Did—did anybody see you?"

"See me? Sure, I guess so. I've been waiting for more than an hour and several people passed by."

"Jeff," she said, backing away, "I can't talk to you! Not tonight!"

I thought I had been pretty patient, considering the things that had happened, but my patience was about used up. I wasn't going to be put off this time.

"All right," she said finally. "But don't let anybody see us, not even Stella."

I took her arm and we stayed in the shadows behind the buildings and after a while we got to that little shack that she called home. Inside, Kate found a match and lit the smoky lamp, then she pulled the flour-sack curtains across the window and turned to me. "All right," she said flatly, "you're here. Now why is it so important that you talk to me?"

"For one thing, I want to know why you slipped that prepared deck in the game yesterday."

She smiled faintly, completely without humor. "Does it make any difference?"

205

Maybe it didn't, but I wanted to know just the same, so I played a hunch. "Kate, are you still in love with McCain? Did he promise again to take you away from here? Is that the reason?"

She said nothing.

"All right, maybe it isn't important. But this is: Why did you give McCain the combination to Stella's safe?"

For a moment her eyes were blank. "What are you talking about?"

"Kate, you've watched Stella open that safe of hers more times than you can count. So you must have known that combination. You're the *only* one who could have known it, for that matter, except Stella herself."

The blank look vanished and her eyes blazed. "You're crazy! Even if I had known the combination, do you think I'd give it to Jay McCain after what he's done to me?"

"Maybe. If you loved him."

"You're crazier than I thought!"

"That might be, but it's the only way it makes sense. Kate, I haven't had an easy time in this town of yours. I've been pistol whipped, shot at, and beaten by the town marshal, to mention a few of the things that have happened to me. I want some answers!"

She seemed to grow smaller as I looked at her. She dropped her head, and not until I saw the lamplight glistening on her cheeks did I realize that she was crying. She walked across the room and sat on the edge of the shabby bed, looking very small.

"Don't you want to tell me about it, Kate?"

All the fight went out of her. "All right." She didn't look up. "I told Jay how to get into the safe. He said he'd kill me if I didn't, because he still thinks I stacked that prepared deck against him."

I heard my breath whistle through my teeth. "Will you tell the Marshal about it, Kate?"

"Jay would kill me! Besides, Silas Mills already knows about it."

I hadn't been ready for that. For one stunned moment I couldn't make a sound. Then, "Do you mean that the Marshal knew all along that McCain was behind the robbery, and he didn't try to do anything about it?"

But she would tell it in her own way and in her own time. There were no tears now. Her eyes were cold and flinty when she looked at me. "I told you the story of my life once," she said, "but you didn't believe it. Do you remember that first night when you bought me the glass of wine? When you fought Jay?"

"I remember."

"The story I told that night was true, most of it. My family did have a little haywire ranch here in the brush country. My father and brother were killed in the war, and my mother died the next year. Most people here in Sabina know the story. You could have checked on it if you'd been interested."

There didn't seem to be any answer to that, so I said nothing.

"I had nothing when I came to Sabina," she went on. "The only person I knew here was Silas Mills. Before the war he had been a friend of my father's. He helped us get started with the ranch; he said this country needed settling by people like us. That's the kind of man he is."

I didn't know where the story was leading, but I was willing to wait it out, now that she had started talking. After a pause, she said, "I told you once that Jay was the only friend I had when I came here. Well, that wasn't true. Silas took me in, he treated me like his own daughter and got me a job in the eating place across the street from Stella's. Jay used to come in there every day. I was just a fool girl, I guess. No man had ever talked to me the way he did, no man could make me feel the way he could by just looking at me. . . ."

"So you left the job that Silas got for you and went to Stella's?"

She nodded. "Do you wonder why I'm tellin' you all this?"

"Because McCain wouldn't marry you and you hope I'll help you even the score?"

She looked as though the thought had never occurred to her. "Even the score?" She smiled bitterly. "I'm sick of Jay, but more than that, I'm sick of myself."

"What is it you want? To see McCain dead?"

"Yes," she said coldly. "I want to see him dead. Not because of what he's done to me, but because of what he's doing to Silas."

In some dark corner of my mind a crazy idea was trying to make itself heard, but it was so ridiculous that I closed the door on it and refused to listen. I said, "What has Silas got to do with it?"

She lifted that stone-cold face and looked at me, but she said nothing. That crazy idea went to work again, and this time I let it in and listened. A full, long minute must have passed before I finally asked the question.

"Kate, is Silas Mills in love with you? Is that what you're trying to say?"

She didn't have to say it. That was the way it had to be. And, as I thought of it, everything was suddenly clear. Well, I'll be damned! I thought quietly. The Marshal in love with a fancy girl!

Well, stranger things had happened, I supposed—and anyway, Kate Masters hadn't been a fancy girl when she first came to Sabina. She had Jay McCain to thank for that.

It was still a little hard to believe, but it explained perfectly all the Marshal's actions that I had wondered about. Silas must have known that Kate had given the safe combination to McCain, and that was the reason he had deliberately let the gambler get away with it. He hadn't wanted to involve the girl!

That, I suppose, was when I first heard the sound that raised the nerve ends to the top of my skin. It was a very small sound and it quickly mingled and became a part of hundreds of other small sounds that live in the night. But I had heard it. There was no mistake about it. It was the tiny silver sound that a spur rowel makes when a foot is moved very carefully, and it came from just the other side of the shack's front door.

Someone was out there. Someone who had no business being out there was finding my conversation with Kate Masters too interesting to suit me.

The girl hadn't heard the sound at all. She looked puzzled as I strained to hear it again. She was just about to ask me about it when I waved her to silence. Then I stepped to the door and jerked it open.

That was a mistake. I should have had my revolver in my hand before I touched that door-latch, but I didn't think about that until it was too late. Slim Kasper had been smarter. His .44 was unholstered and I must have stepped right into it. I could feel the hard muzzle of the gun in my belly before I could see who was holding it.

I was a flick of an eye from death. Either he would pull the trigger or he wouldn't, and there was not a thing that I could do about it. I heard the surprised whistle of breath between his teeth. He stood there for what could not possibly have been more than a split second, but it was a lifetime for me. And then he said, unsmiling now, "Just don't move, Denfield."

He rammed the muzzle harder into my midsection and expertly lifted my revolver from its holster. "Now get back inside," he said coldly.

It happened fast. Kate Masters didn't know what was happening until I backed into the room with Kasper following like a shadow. "Get back there against the wall, Denfield, and just stand there. I've got a little decision to make." He smiled then, for the first time.

The situation wasn't of Kasper's making, and it wasn't the way he would have liked it, but he was too good a gambler to let one hand break him. The girl hadn't made a sound until now, but when I looked at her I could almost see the scream working its way into her throat.

"Don't make me do it, Kate," Kasper said, turning my revolver in her direction. The scream died before it was born. "That's better," he said.

He shoved his own revolver into his holster and kept mine in his hand. He spoke to Kate now, watching me from the corner of his eye.

"I wouldn't like to be in your shoes, Kate," he said softly. "McCain didn't like it when you switched him a cold deck. He didn't like it at all. He's goin' to like it even less when he learns

211

you've been blabberin' all you know to Denfield!"

He laughed suddenly, feeling that he had complete control of the situation. "And you," he went on, looking at me. "You had to keep playin' even when you knew the game was rigged, didn't you, Denfield? Well, you know what happens to a man when he plays in a rigged game. He loses, Denfield."

I could guess what was going on in his mind. There was still a good chance that he and McCain could bluff Kate into silence, but he would have no such ideas about me. A business end of a gun was the way to take care of me. I could see the idea working behind his eyes; he was tasting it, savoring it, and finding it to his liking . . . when Kate Masters leaped at him.

I hadn't expected it and neither had Slim Kasper. With a small sound in her throat she leaped catlike at McCain's sideman and I could see the startled look of disbelief in the gambler's eyes. His reaction was instinctive, and completely without emotion. He simply pulled the trigger.

In Kasper's hand, my old Griswold and Grier exploded with shocking impact. The sound mushroomed inside the shack, seemed to bulge the flimsy walls outward. Kate Masters leaned forward as the bullet hit her, as though she were trying desperately to force herself past this small obstacle and get on with her determined business of clawing Kasper's face. I don't think she ever fully realized what had happened. Her mouth still worked in helpless rage as she fell to her knees. Then a puzzled expression clouded her eyes as she tried vainly to reach the gambler with one outstretched hand. At last she fell over on her side, shaking her head in bewilderment, still not understanding.

And that was the way Kate Masters died.

I was on my knees beside her and for a moment I had completely forgotten Slim Kasper. There was nothing I could do. Nothing anyone could do. By the time I reached her she was dead. She was a sprawled, unpretty heap on the floor, the soiled ruffles of her doxie's dress now soaking up the spreading crimson. I thought for one terrible moment that I was going to be sick, for I had never seen a woman killed like that before. There was a coldness inside me as I thought:

Good-by, Kate. Wherever you are now, I hope it's a better place than the one you just left.

Only a few seconds had passed since Kasper had pulled the trigger. As I knelt there, it seemed that the sound of the explosion still crashed about the flimsy walls of the shack, and I wondered if I would ever stop hearing it. When I looked up at last, Slim Kasper had not moved. Realization showed in his eyes, then a beginning of horror, and finally desperation. I knew then that the gambler was aware of how Silas Mills felt about the girl. At that moment Slim Kasper was seeing himself as good as dead. The Marshal would kill him for this if it was the last thing he ever did.

I made no move yet, for killing me could not possibly make his chances of survival any worse. Slim Kasper was scared, plenty scared, as he began backing toward the door. He couldn't take his eyes off the dead girl, although he kept that revolver aimed at me. Someone was sure to have heard the shot. There was panic in Kasper's eyes. Someone, possibly the Marshal himself, was surely on his way to see what the shooting was about.

Then, just as he reached the door, I saw something happen to those eyes of his. He dragged in a quick gulp of air, and the sudden panic drained out of him. For a moment he stared at me and almost grinned. Slim Kasper had just figured out a way to keep his head out of a hangman's noose.

"Stand up," he said tightly. Wondering why he wasn't running for his life, I stood up, for there was nothing else to do. "All right," he grinned, "move over here by the door."

We could hear the commotion now, the pounding of boot heels and the shouting as the Sabina citizens who were still up tried to locate the spot where the shot had come from. Then, at that moment, I understood what Kasper was up to. As I moved toward the door, he pulled his own revolver from his holster and threw my old

Griswold and Grier on the floor beside the dead girl. That old Griswold and Grier with one exploded cartridge in the cylinder! *My gun!*

Now I knew why Kasper was grinning. Plenty of people knew that gun. It was probably the only one of its kind in Sabina County. It was the gun that had killed Kate Masters, and that was all Silas Mills would need to know.

Chapter Fifteen

Sometimes a man has to do crazy things to stay alive, and that was the reason I did what I did next. The pound of boot heels was getting closer and the musical sound of spurs was beginning to sound like a funeral dirge. I stepped to one side of the door, and, like a rattler's head, the muzzle of that revolver followed me. The next move was the big gamble. I was betting that Kasper wouldn't fire his own revolver if he could possibly help it, for if his gun had also been fired, it would cloud the evidence against me. Like betting into two aces, it was not a good gamble and the odds were against me, but it was a chance that a gambler has to take sometimes. I jumped back in the opposite direction and slashed at Kasper's wrist with the edge of my hand.

My hunch had been right. Kasper had plenty of time to swing that revolver around and, at point-blank range, put a bullet through my heart. But that wasn't the way he wanted it. One shot had been fired and it had come from my Griswold and Grier, and that was the way he wanted to keep it. Bluffing is a bad way to gamble, but when you bluff and win there is a tremendous satisfaction in it, and that was the way I felt now. When Kasper didn't shoot me immediately, I knew that he wasn't going to shoot me at all.

He tried to bring his gun hand up high enough to take a swing at my head, but I had already cracked his wrist by that time. He let out a bellow of rage and clawed at me as his revolver crashed to the floor. He tried to hold me by wrestling, but nothing but a bullet could have held me then. I shoved him back against the wall and ran.

Where do you go from here, Denfield?

There seemed to be no place to go. Kasper had come out of the shack by now and was yelling curses. And out of the darkness, directly in front of me, three men were running in my direction. Two of them I guessed were the cow hands I had seen standing in front of the saloon. There was no guessing about the third one. He was Silas Mills.

Doesn't he ever rest or sleep? I thought grimly. Is he *always* on the job?

So it seemed, but I didn't have time to wonder about it. I skidded in the loose gravel as I changed directions and began running toward the other end of Main Street. Where I was going, I didn't know. I just knew that I couldn't stand there and try to explain to the Marshal that I hadn't killed Kate Masters. He would take one look at that pistol of mine and ask questions after the funeral. My funeral!

"Stay where you are!" I heard Mills bellow. "Stop!"

Not if I can help it! I thought. I headed for the deep shadows behind Sabina's business buildings, and Mills began yelling again. He fired once, twice with his revolver, but I didn't hear the bullets and I guessed that he was firing well over my head in warning. Well, I thought, pretty soon he won't be firing over my head. He'll be shooting to kill as soon as Kasper puts a few things together for him.

Now I heard Mills giving orders to the two cow hands to follow me, and I knew that he would head for Kate Masters' shack to see what the trouble had been in the first place. That would be the beginning of the end unless I could get out of Sabina. Far away from Sabina. And that didn't seem possible.

I could hear the two cow hands pounding behind me, but they seemed to have lost heart for the chase. After all, this wasn't their argument. For all they knew, I had a gun and was ready to shoot the first one to come within range. And in that darkness, there was no way of knowing whether you were in range or not.

They dropped farther behind as I slipped between buildings and hit the plank walk of Main Street. Then I saw my chance to get away. My chance to live a few hours longer, maybe, if I was especially lucky. The two horses dozing at the hitching rack in front of Stella's saloon probably belonged to the two cow hands that were supposed to be chasing me. I picked out the one that looked the biggest and strongest and hit the saddle in one jump. He was a big, sleek-looking black with a white blaze and white forestockings; some cowboy's pride and joy.

But the big animal wasn't used to having strangers hitting him all at once like that, like a sack of coal hitting the saddle, and he wanted to buck. I got him calmed down before the cow hands rounded the corner into the street, then I leaned over and untied the other horse, and gave him a smart crack across the rump. He gave a startled snort and spurted up the street in the direction of Kansas.

That was when the first cow hand rounded into the street. "Hey!" he yelled. "By God, that's my horse you're on, mister!"

I just hoped it was the only horse around at that hour. I shot my boot heels into the black's ribs and the big animal exploded into a dead run. We were well past the public corral, Sabina falling behind us, when I realized that it was hopeless to think that I could get far without a gun.

It was time for another gamble. I was beginning to get sick of the word, sick of taking crazy chances, but there was very little I had to say about it now. I had to have a gun. In the back of my mind a plan was taking shape, the only plan possible. Somehow I had to get my hands on Slim Kasper and choke the truth out of him before Silas Mills settled everything by putting a bullet into me. If I couldn't get Kasper, I would have to settle for McCain. But I sure couldn't handle him without a gun. There were some doubts that I could do it *with* one. Anyway, the time for another gamble had come. I had to go back to Sabina.

There was only one man who could help me now, and that was Phil Carney. The thought wasn't very comforting, but I was in no position to choose my allies.

I was hoping that the Marshal, in his blind anger and grief, would come straight after me after the cow hands had pointed out the direction, the way a fighting bull, blinded by pain, follows the cape and lets the man go. Still I rode straight ahead for another full minute or so until Sabina was well behind me, and finally I turned that black horse back on himself, circling around to the west. If everything went according to plan, I would reenter the town from the opposite direction. I would rouse Phil Carney out of bed, get myself a gun and maybe a grub sack, and hope that he would explain the business to Laura and somehow manage to keep the Marshal off my tail for a while.

It was a big order. Too big an order to trust to a kid like Carney, I thought. For an instant I was tempted to double back again and head straight for McCain and take my chances with my bare hands.

That particular bit of insanity didn't last long. I would have to take my chances with the kid, whether I liked it or not. Anyway, I didn't like the idea of leaving town in the middle of the night, letting Laura hear the story about Kate Masters secondhand.

It was rough country, that land west of Sabina, but the white moon was a help now, and the black horse was sure-footed and fast. There was a good chance that the whole town was roused out of its sleep by now, but I doubted that Silas Mills had stayed behind to gather up a posse. Not this time.

I put my horse into a dry wash and we followed it for maybe a half mile, and finally we came out of the gully and hit the wagon road that I was looking for. I stuck to the road now because it was faster and I didn't expect to see anybody on it—and pretty soon I could see Sabina.

At first I thought the place was on fire. There was a reddish haze along the rooftops and a dozen or more dancing flames in the street, and finally I realized that the lights were torches and lanterns. The town was roused up, all right. I could see sudden orange lights appearing in windows, and then more dancing lights entered the street as the menfolk began to gather. I glanced up at the moon, feeling a coldness in the pit of my stomach. I thought: A great night for a lynching!

By now I was in sight of the Charleston House. I nudged the black horse around the back way and jumped out of the saddle on the far side of the house. A lamp was just being lighted in an upstairs room, and then another light flared in the downstairs parlor as I went around the back way and tried the door.

I almost ran into Mrs. Lorring, who was just coming into the kitchen.

"What on earth, Capt'n Denfield! What's all the noise?"

She was huge and bleary-eyed, as shapeless as a cotton bale in her enormous white wrapper. I said, "I'm going to take a look now. Is Phil up in his room?"

"Why, I suppose . . ." But I was already in the other room by now, hitting the stairs three at a time. Then Laura appeared at the foot of the stairs.

"Jeff, what is it?"

"Don't go out of the house, Laura." I wanted to explain, but there was no time. I pushed the door open just as Phil Carney was about to come out.

"What the hell's goin' on?" he said. "Have you been outside?"

"Plenty is going on!" I stepped inside and closed

the door. "A woman was killed a while ago. They think I did it."

He looked at me as though he hadn't understood the words. "A woman? Killed?"

"Kate Masters, the girl that worked in Stella's saloon. Slim Kasper shot her. With my gun. I haven't got time to go into it, but anyway, Silas Mills is bound to think I did it as soon as he finds that revolver."

"You *left* it there? That old Griswold and Grier?"

"That's what I'm trying to tell you," I said impatiently. "I was lucky to get away myself."

Stunned, he shook his head, but, for once, he didn't ask questions. "This is bad. This is just as bad as a thing can get, if Mills really thinks you did it. I never heard of a woman bein' killed in this part of Texas. It just doesn't happen, even to a saloon girl. They'll hang you in a minute."

"I'm well aware of that."

Since I had walked through the door, Phil Carney seemed to have aged five years. "Christ!" he said, rubbing his face. "I'm sorry, Jeff. I shouldn't have got you into this mess."

"If Mills catches me, you can be sorry then. Right now I want a revolver and a rifle and a small grub sack. And some ammunition."

He shook his head. "You'll never get away by yourself. I'll go with you; I know this country."

"I'm not going far," I said. "Just until I find McCain or Kasper."

Until now he hadn't tied the two together. McCain and Kate Masters' death. He said, with a bit too much calm, "Do you think McCain had anything to do with the killing?"

"Not directly, maybe. But he sure sent Kasper in to watch her, because Kate was in on the robbery and McCain was afraid she might give the thing away."

But he was thinking ahead of me now. He only nodded.

I said, "Whatever you're thinking, forget it. I'm in this alone."

He didn't even look at me. He walked out of the room and down the hall, and in a minute he was back with two revolvers and a rifle. "These will have to do," he said. "Laura's fixin' grub sacks for us."

"Did you tell her?"

He glanced at me, then at the window. "I didn't have to. They're yellin' it in the streets. That you killed Kate Masters."

"Does Laura believe that?"

He looked at me again, coldly. "I reckon she wouldn't be fixin' the grub sacks if she did."

I felt better, in spite of the angry gabbling that drifted into the room from Main Street. I buckled on one revolver while the kid slung his own cartridge belt around his waist. The angry muttering began to grow louder as more citizens gathered, and I decided that there simply wasn't time to argue with the kid about whether or not he was going with me. Anyway, maybe it was his fight as much as mine, now that we knew for sure where the money had gone.

We went down the stairs and past Mrs. Lorring, who was standing in the middle of the empty parlor wringing her hands. "Capt'n Denfield . . . Phil . . ." But we went on past and into the kitchen, where Laura was wrapping leftover biscuits and side meat in a newspaper. Without looking up, she put the package into a small sugar sack and said, "Phil, you go out front and try to keep them away from the house until Jeff gets away."

I expected an argument, but he only said, "All right." Then, to me, "I have to get a horse anyway. I can pick up one at the corral, probably. Do you know where the south wagon road bends off to the west?"

"I know the place."

"I'll meet you there." He was already heading for the front door.

Laura turned, holding the grub sack out to me. She stood there, pale, barefoot, wearing one of those white wrappers that all women seemed to wear at times like this. "Jeff . . ." Her face had been almost expressionless until that moment. Now a grimness set itself at the corners of her mouth. "Jeff, you've got to go! There isn't much time!"

I took her shoulders and held her against me. "I know," I said. "Don't worry."

Don't worry!

"Jeff," she said, "Phil knows this country well. He can take you south, across the border, and you'll be safe there. You can make your way back East."

I had no way of knowing what her brother had told her. It hadn't occurred to me that she thought I was running, leaving Sabina for good. Well, I thought, maybe it's better this way. What she doesn't know won't worry her. Not now, anyway. I held her very close, and for a moment I was tempted to test her. I wanted to say, "Will you come with me, Laura? Will you leave your brother and the ranch and everything else behind and come with me?" I wanted to say it, but I didn't. Maybe I was afraid of what the answer would be.

And that was the way I left her. I walked out of the kitchen and out of the house, and she stood there very erect, her head up. Still proud. Not forgetting for an instant that she was a Carney. For all she knew, I was walking out on her, leaving her exactly the way I had found her, or worse. But there was no whimper from her, no attempt to hold me. In a way it was frustrating to know that she was so completely self-sufficient—but I was proud of her, too. Headstrong, proud, confident, but she was for me and I knew there would never be another.

Good-by, Laura.

But there was no sound from the house. I made

my way around to the horse and lashed the grub sack down with the saddle leathers. There was still a great deal of milling and confusion in the street, but now the angry procession seemed to be headed up toward the public corral. Now, I decided, was the time to make my break.

I led the black horse behind the Charleston House and mounted there. We left town the back way, as quietly as possible, just about the time the new posse began pounding to the north after the Marshal. Maybe I had thrown them off the trail for a while, but not for long. Silas Mills was not a man to stay fooled for long. I put iron to the black horse and he settled down to a ground-eating run, heading toward the south wagon road.

Phil Carney was waiting at the bend when I got there. He was astride a rangy, deep-chested bay that was rigged out with a boot for the saddle gun. "I had a hell of a time gettin' a horse," Carney said. "Seemed like every man in Sabina was tryin' to raid the public corral." His mouth stretched in a thin, humorless grin. "They're carryin' enough rope to hang a regiment of men. A fancy girl gets mighty important around here after she's dead."

I wondered what Kate Masters would have said to all the commotion her death had caused. She had had a sense of humor once, but I doubted that this would have amused her.

I said, "What about the Marshal?"

"Mills? Looks like he bit at the bait you threw

out, but I wouldn't depend on his swallowing it altogether."

I was thinking the same thing. "We'd better get off the road," I said, reining the horse around. "Can you show me how to get to McCain's place from here?"

The kid's eyebrows went up a little. "You can't just ride in on McCain. He's sure to have his men staked out all around the headquarters buildings."

"That's a chance I'll have to take. Right now I'd rather face a dozen of McCain's men than just one of Silas Mills."

He pulled his bay around, gazing off into the fading moonlight. "Yeah," he said softly, "I guess you're right." He looked at me. "It's now or never, isn't it?"

"It looks like it."

And he was right. His play for that ranch would be over for good if the Marshal found him with me now. Helping a "woman-killer" escape would finish him in Sabina, Carney or no Carney. I thought about that now with a strange objectivity, wondering if he would drop me, now that I had become a liability to him. The smartest thing he could do was show me the way to the border and wash his hands of the affair, chalk up his big gamble to experience, and start figuring out some other way to wheedle that ranch out of McCain.

But he didn't hesitate when he said, "Well, we'd better ride."

Chapter Sixteen

"There it is," Phil Carney said, pointing to a distant cluster of shapeless shadows. The while moon had long since settled behind a gauzy bank of drifting clouds, and only occasionally did it come out long enough to give us a glimpse of the brush-strewn wilderness through which we were riding. "Those are the headquarters buildings," he said tightly. "My ranch."

I thought: McCain's ranch, you mean. But I didn't say it. The important thing was that we had finally reached it without getting shot and without running into the Marshal or his posse. Then, even as we peered through the darkness, the front of the ranch house came alive with light.

Carney made a sound of surprise. "They couldn't have spotted us at this distance."

I thought I knew what had happened. "Slim Kasper must have cut himself away from the Marshal," I said. "I'd almost forgotten how important Kate Masters was to McCain. If she was killed he'd be sure to want to hear about it, and that's why Kasper came tearing back to the ranch."

It was all guesswork, of course, but everything seemed to fit together. Then I thought of something else, something not very pleasant. It just occurred to me that McCain would find it absolutely necessary to find me and have me killed. It wasn't very likely that I could get to Silas Mills and convince him that I had nothing to do with Kate Masters' death—but if I *could,* all the blame would land eventually in McCain's lap. I was the one man who had even a remote chance to ruin him, and McCain wasn't a man to take chances, no matter how remote they were. I had learned that the hard way.

I felt Phil Carney watching me, and I knew instinctively that he had been thinking in the same direction. Across the brush, one after another of the ranch buildings came to life. Windows opened like cat eyes in the darkness, bright orange with lamplight. Soon lighted lanterns were swinging across the ranch yard as men hustled to corrals and outbuildings.

"McCain will probably throw his men in with the posse," I said. "There'll be a hanging on the spot if they find me, and anybody with me will probably get the same. You'd better deal yourself out of this, kid, before things get hotter than they already are."

He said one word, a savage expression of disgust that I hadn't heard since I was a part of the Confederate Army. Then he nodded to the west, where the dim crest of a ridge stood knifelike against the night. "There's one thing sure, we're not goin' to surprise anybody now. But we can ride over there and maybe get a better look at what McCain's up to."

It took only a few minutes to pull back and come up behind the ridge. As we looked down now we could see that the lights had taken on a kind of order, and I guessed that McCain had gathered the men together for instructions.

I said, "How many men on McCain's payroll?"

"Maybe a dozen, countin' the ones ridin' line. It looks like he's got the whole crew out down there."

The kid and I were thinking along the same lines again. It was a long chance, but if McCain pulled his crew out of there to join the Marshal's posse, there would be nothing to stop us from going in and having a look at the place—just in case that stolen money might be hidden in the ranch house. Of course, that money couldn't help me much now, but at least it might give the posse something to think about if they caught us, if we could prove that McCain or his men had broken into Stella's. I had a hunch that Phil Carney wasn't interested in that angle so much. It was the money itself that he wanted, and to hell with worrying about the posse.

In spite of the situation, in spite of what had happened to me in Sabina, I felt myself grinning faintly. To hell with tomorrow. To hell with every-thing but what was happening right now. I could almost believe that the war had never ended and we were once again a part of that rag, tag, and bobtail outfit that General Hood had called an army.

"By God," the kid whispered, as though he were holding his breath. "There they go."

Sure enough, we could hear the pound of hoofs as those shapeless shadows of men and horses crossed the big ranch yard. Pretty soon we couldn't see them, but we could still hear the horses and they were headed toward Sabina.

Carney said, "Do you think they'll hook up with Mills?"

"That's what I'd do if I was McCain. He isn't going to get mixed up in a woman killing if he can help it, and the surest way to get out of it is to hang it onto somebody else."

"And it looks like you're elected," he said wearily. Phil Carney sat very erect in the saddle, staring up at the flying clouds. After a long pause he said, "I can still get you to the border."

I looked at him. "No, thanks."

"This is my fight now. There's no reason for you to sit in."

"I don't figure it that way," I said. "Remember that whipping I took that first night in Sabina? Remember that neat way McCain tried to murder me in your front yard?"

So much time passed that I thought he wasn't going to answer. Then he said, "I remember. But I don't think those things would hold you here if it wasn't for Laura."

I don't know why, but there was something in the way he said it that started an old anger boiling. "Don't you think that's my business?"

"Maybe not," he said flatly. "I'm not exactly blind. I don't know what my sister has told you, but I've seen the way she's been makin' up to you. Forget her, Jeff. That's the best thing you can do; just forget her and get as far away from Sabina as possible."

I said roughly, "I think you've said about enough."

His head snapped around. "I haven't said nearly enough, that's the trouble. When I started it all back in Virginia, I never figured it would wind up like this. I figured that picture you had in your mind wouldn't look so good once you got to know my sister as she really was. But I underestimated Laura. That can be fatal, Jeff, underestimating a woman like her."

Suddenly he laughed, the sound grating on my nerves. But, for some reason, I didn't stop him. "Do you think she meant the things she told you?" he asked shortly. "Don't you think she told McCain the same things when she thought he could help her? She's my sister, but I know her, Jeff. Don't forget that. She's a Carney, just as I am, and that's what she'll always be. Look at that ranch down there. It means everything to me, it's the only purpose in life that I have, because it's a part of the Carney name and without it the name is incomplete. Well, that's the way Laura feels about it too, I guess. Why else would she agree to marry a man like McCain? Why, for that matter, would she be making a play for a professional gambler like you, when the best men in Sabina would marry her in a minute? Look—"

That's as far as he got. I reached out and grabbed the front of his shirt, almost jerking him out of the saddle. "That's enough!" I hardly recognized the voice as my own.

He offered no resistance. "All right, Jeff. I should have known better than to talk about it."

I let him go. But what he had said had shaken me, and the rage inside me was slow to settle. Something in the back of my mind told me that maybe he was right and I was still playing the fool. It was a part I was good at; I'd had enough practice.

I very carefully covered the idea up and stowed it away in the darkest corner of my mind and tried to forget it. I breathed deeply of the night air and gave myself a chance to settle down, and finally I said:

"McCain probably left his wrangler behind, and maybe a cook, but it looks like most of them are gone."

"I reckon," the kid said flatly, "that a wrangler and a cook won't stop us from lookin' around."

With no more talk, we nudged our horses and moved down the slope. I motioned Phil Carney to

233

follow me, and we circled the main building as quietly as possible, so that we could come into the place from the direction that McCain had just followed. There was no way of telling just how much of a chance we were taking, but it seemed reasonable to assume that the Carney gold was hidden somewhere inside that ranch house, and getting it back was worth any chance we might be taking. Maybe I could even bargain for my life with it, if that posse caught up with us.

We were getting close now, and most of the lights were still blazing in the main house and outbuildings. I held out a hand and said, "Hold it a minute." A figure of a man came around the far side of the house, from the barns, and he was standing near the front porch peering into the darkness.

"Jay, is that you?"

Phil Carney pulled alongside me. "Let him guess," he said.

"Slim?" the voice called.

We rode on until we were almost touching the lighted area in front of the house. I could see now that the man was an old-timer, gray and grizzled, clad only in long underwear and boots. The wrangler, all right, or the cook, because he was too stove up to work as a regular rider. He was coming toward us now, favoring his right leg as he walked.

"Who's out there?"

The kid had his revolver in his hand. He rode into the ring of light and almost had the muzzle in the old man's face before he knew what was happening.

The old-timer grunted, more surprised than scared. "What the hell is this? Say, you're the Carney kid!"

"That's right, old man," the kid said quietly. "Now just don't move and you'll be all right. Is there anybody here with you?"

I was still in the darkness and the old man was still trying to make me out. Carney had to ask the question again.

The oldster spat at the ground, seemingly unconcerned. "Nah, I'm the only one here. Jay and Slim took the rest of the boys and headed for Sabina, so they said." He squinted harder. "Is that that river-gamblin' jasper you got back there with you?"

I said, "Keep him quiet for a few minutes while I scout around the barns." I touched the black horse and rode around to the side of the house and then around to the nearest barn, where a hanging lantern was still burning. Nothing there. Nothing around the corrals but a few horses that had been brought up for the next morning's work. I rode back to the front of the house and said, "It looks like McCain took everybody with him, all right."

The kid put his revolver away. "The old man here says he works as both wrangler and cook."

"He must be telling the truth. Did he say how long he expects McCain to be away?"

The wrangler spat again. "Didn't say because I don't know. I'll tell you one thing, though. You'll catch hell if he comes back and finds you plunderin' around his place."

"That's a chance we'll have to take," the kid said dryly, dropping out of the saddle. We hitched at the rack on the near side of the house and herded the old man ahead of us, up to the front porch. It occurred to me then that I had hardly given any attention at all to this ranch that had given me so much trouble. According to the kid, I was now standing on sacred ground, Carney ground, but it felt pretty much like any other ground to me. From what I could see of it, there were two pretty good-sized barns and a few sheds and corrals; except for the ranch house itself, that was about all there was to it. There was no great difference between this place and a hundred other ranches, although this one might be a bit more run down than some others.

The ranch house was not a big one—five, maybe six rooms—built of split pulp logs, the cracks filled with what looked to be a mixture of red clay and slake mortar. All the buildings needed paint or a coat of whitewash, and the pole corrals needed mending. Looking at it, I couldn't understand how it could be so important to a man, to a community. Of course, I couldn't see beyond the headquarters buildings themselves; I couldn't see the thousands of acres of belly-high grass that grew in the gullies and washes of that wild country, and I couldn't see the fattening cattle that grazed there, and I couldn't imagine what the owner's bankbook would look like after he had deposited the money that those cattle would bring.

I couldn't see, and what I couldn't see I couldn't understand, and anyway I had no wish to understand right now. My main interest was in keeping my head out of a noose as long as possible. If I could just get my hands on the gold that had been taken from Stella Taggart's safe, if I could somehow prove to the good citizens of Sabina that I had nothing to do with the robbery or the killing, maybe I would have a chance. But not much of one, even then.

As we went single file up the front steps, across the porch, and into the house itself, I thought: Be smart, Denfield. It's still not too late to get to the border.

But I didn't say it.

The three of us now stood in the center of the front room, a big room with a big Mexican-style fireplace in the corner about two feet off the floor. The old wrangler stood scratching and blinking, only mildly interested in what we were up to. "You know," he said, "this is the first time I was ever in this room. Been in the back rooms plenty of times, but never here. Can't say," he grunted, "that it's so much. Looks pretty skimpy to me."

Skimpy was the word for it. The room was

almost bare, but it didn't seem to bother Phil Carney. He stood apart from us, lost for the moment in his own private world of what used to be and what could have been and, probably, what was going to be. He walked quickly into another room, and another, and I think that he had forgotten, for the moment, about the money that we had come to look for. I followed him into a room that looked to be an office of some kind. Probably the place where the ranch books were kept. As he stood in the center of the room, the kid's eyes were alive, more alive than I had ever seen them before.

"My office," he said quietly, speaking to no one in particular. "My father built this house with his own hands. This room."

I was already beginning to go through the drawers of a roll-top desk when the explosion of sound seemed to split the night wide open.

It was a rifle, a big rifle or maybe a musket, and the sound came from outside the house, from the direction of the barns. Phil Carney wheeled sharply, jarred abruptly from that dream world of his.

"McCain! They've come back!"

I didn't think so. Not yet, anyway. By that time I was in the front room, and since I was already beginning to appreciate our incredible blunder, I was not surprised to find the room empty. The old wrangler was gone. Well, I thought bitterly, if we die tonight on the nearest tree, we'll have nobody to blame but ourselves!

Phil Carney was right behind me as I kicked the front door open and hit the porch. The night exploded again, and I saw the fire fly this time, and the mushroom of powder smoke, and I knew that our string of luck had finally played out. I could see the old wrangler now, standing in front of the lighted barn, working frantically with a ramrod. The musket he had between his legs had a barrel as long as a hoe handle, and from the noise it made I judged it to be at least a .56 caliber or more.

We ran across the ranch yard toward the barn. It seemed to me that the noise that old musket made could surely be heard all the way to Sabina, and maybe it could. There was one thing we could depend on: It could be heard by McCain and his men. And it wouldn't take them long to figure out that something was happening back at the ranch that needed looking into.

The kid, running hard alongside me, had his revolver in his hand. "Goddamn him!" he grated. "I'll kill the old sonofabitch for this!"

And then a bit of reason began nudging the panic aside. I said, "That'll do no good. McCain's already heard those shots." Then I saw the old man duck back into the barn, and in another second the long barrel of that musket appeared around the door. We were so close that, when the old man pulled the trigger, the muzzle blast seemed to spew fire in our faces. There was no time for warning. There was just time to throw my body across the kid's legs and both of us went crashing to the ground. We could hear the savage hiss as the lead ball ripped the air over our heads and slammed into the side of the house behind us.

Phil Carney lifted himself to one knee. "By God," he said hoarsely, "that's one act he won't live long enough to regret! While the old bastard reloads, we'll see how he likes some of his own medicine!"

There was no time to argue my cause. I only knew that shooting the old man would be absolutely useless, and I grabbed the kid's hand and took the pistol away from him before his anger had a chance to run away with him. I said, "If you want to live long enough to use this on somebody that counts, you'd better get around to the other side of the house and find your horse."

He was mad, but not so mad that he couldn't think. "I guess you're right." He picked himself up. "But let's get out of here before that wrangler has time to reload that goddamn cannon!"

We got out. We were on the other side of the house and in the saddle before the old-timer let go again with his musket. We forgot about him. He had already done all the damage he could do, and it had been plenty. We put iron to our horses and lit out the back way, around sheds and corrals and bunkhouses, and I was glad that the place was not fenced, for it was dark now. Much too dark for the kind of riding we would have to do.

"It's your play now," I called as we left the headquarters buildings behind. He said nothing, but that little bay of his spurted up ahead and I moved the black behind him, into the dusty drag. I didn't know this country, I had no idea where we were going, but Phil Carney seemed to know. He raced the bay at a breakneck pace through the darkness. He took heart-stopping chances in that wild country of gullies and brush, chances that no sane man would take even in daylight, but I kept the black close to the bay's tail because there seemed to be nothing else to do. I thought: If our luck has really played out, we'll know it soon!

And we did.

The bay misjudged a gully jump in the darkness, probably didn't even see it, and went crashing down directly in front of my black.

But that big black was a good horse. He was sure-footed and strong, and he must have been a wonderful cutting animal, because he somehow managed to miss the bay and make the jump at the same time. And when I doubled him back on himself to see if the kid was still alive, that horse took it in stride.

The bay was dead. It had probably never even felt the hurt of hitting the ground, because it had landed on its neck and its spine had snapped. Phil

Carney had been luckier. That incredible luck of his was still holding, and he managed to postpone the end for a while by coming out of the saddle clean and landing in the heavy buffalo grass in the bottom of the gully. He was already on his feet by the time I reined up.

"Are you all right?" I asked.

"Sure. How about my horse?"

"Dead," I said. "It looks like we ride double from here on out. Which probably won't be long, because McCain is already on our tail by now."

"To hell with McCain," he said tightly. "He's still got a job of work cut out for him." He pointed into the darkness. "Over there somewhere is a place called Mexican's Cave. McCain will think about it for a while before he tries to smoke us out of there."

But it wasn't McCain I was worried about. I was still thinking of Silas Mills.

Chapter Seventeen

Mexican's Cave wasn't a cave at all, it turned out, but a kind of tunnel, a freakish formation in that ragged land caused by the combined forces of erosion and weather. It wasn't much of a fortress, but it would have to do, because that black horse was done for by the time we reached it.

It was almost sunup by the time we got there. That surprised me some and made me wonder where the night had gone to. Before long the pale underbelly of the eastern horizon became shot with bloody red, and I thought: You might as well enjoy it, Denfield. Maybe it's the last sunrise you'll ever see.

"Wonder what's holdin' McCain," Phil Carney said. "He must have picked up our trail by now." He was sitting with his back against the clay bank of the tunnel. Both ends of the formation were open. We were protected on the north and south, but we were sitting ducks for anybody drawing a bead on us from the east or west.

I said, "We can worry about McCain when he gets here. Right now we'd better start throwing up a breastwork of some kind."

Without speaking, we began piling up rocks at both ends of the tunnel. About a hundred yards away I could see that black horse, too weak to move or do anything but shake. Too tired to bow his head and look for graze. Some cow hand was going to be mighty mad about the way we had treated his horse, but he wasn't going to feel much worse about it than I did.

And then we heard the distant pound of hoofs.

Phil Carney said nothing. He piled his last rock in front of the cave, picked up the rifle that he had brought, and checked the loading. Suddenly, as the sound grew louder, he came erect.

"Great God!" he said. "Look at them!"

Not until now had the kid really come around to figuring the odds against us. I had figured them and was not surprised, exactly, but there was a certain shock that came when my figures developed into real men and horses and guns. They came out of the gray western morning, across the bleak brushland; there must have been twenty of them, at least. In the van rode Marshal Silas Mills.

I took a deep breath, tasting every cool particle of the morning air. McCain doesn't bother me, I thought. McCain is just a gambler and gamblers are people I understand. McCain is little, he's nothing, he's less than nothing. But Silas Mills won't rest or sleep or eat until I'm dead!

I don't know what Phil Carney thought about as he watched them come on, but I thought of Laura. It was a rotten thing to have it end like this, without knowing for sure if she had really meant the things she had said, or if, as the kid had said, I had been playing the fool. I had done so many damn-fool things that I hated the thought of doing one more, the last one, the biggest damn-fool thing a man could do: getting himself killed because of a woman.

Just beyond rifle range the horsemen stopped. They had seen that black horse and knew that we were there. Then part of the group broke away and circled wide around, and the man in the lead was McCain.

"This is a nice place you picked out for us," I said dryly. "McCain is bringing his boys around to get on the other side."

"If you don't like it here," the kid said, "you can move out into the open."

Silas Mills remained motionless, giving the gambler time to get into position. Then he lifted his arm and moved his own men around until they were out of sight, blocked out by the clay wall of our cave. There was nothing to do but wait and wonder why I hadn't made for the border while there still had been time.

"Carney!" Silas Mills's big voice boomed across the wasteland. "Come out with your hands up, Carney, and you won't be bothered. I'll see to it personally."

The kid jacked a cartridge into his rifle.

"This is your last chance, Carney! I want that partner of yours, not you!"

I looked at him and he made no move at all. He was sitting again with his back to the clay wall.

I said, "Don't be a fool. Do as the Marshal says."

"If the Marshal wants me, let him come and get me!"

Mills's voice boomed again. "I'm not askin' you again, Carney!"

"Go to hell!" the kid yelled.

For a few moments the morning was heavy with dead silence. At last I stood up, trying to get the words straight in my mind. "This kind of thing was all right, maybe, during the war," I said. "But there's not much sense in being a hero now. It serves no purpose."

"It serves my purpose," he said with that same flatness. Then he looked at me, and his eyes were older, much older than they had been a few minutes before. "I wanted somethin'," he said, "and I didn't care how I got it. But maybe I'm not so tough as I thought I was. Sure, I could walk out now and save my skin, but afterward I'd hate to live with myself, and I don't think I could do it."

There seemed to be nothing to say to that. He had gambled and he had lost, and now was the time for paying up. It seemed that Phil Carney had grown into a man at last, the kind of man that the Carney name seemed to stand for around here. But too late to do him any good. Well, I thought, a man may be a lot of things in his lifetime, and he may do a lot of things that aren't very commendable, but it's not up to somebody else to tell him how he ought to die.

The cave was very quiet. Phil Carney's jaw was set and he wasn't going to be moved. A gentle breeze moaned softly across the brushland. Outside, we could hear the Marshal getting his men where he wanted them, and I thought: Well, it could have happened many times before, behind some bloody hedge or rock wall in Virginia. I've been living on borrowed time and maybe I ought to recognize it.

But the thought held little consolation.

"Denfield!" It was the Marshal's voice again, and it came as a surprise to me, because I'd figured he was through talking. "Denfield!" The word was diamond-hard and bitter. "Come out of there and . . . I'll see that you get a trial in Sabina."

The words came with great reluctance and only a few people knew how much the promise had cost him. But being a lawman, I guess, gets into a man's blood. And if he is a good lawman, his duty comes above all things. Even above hate and grief. And Silas Mills was a good lawman.

I knew that Phil Carney was watching me, but I didn't look at him. I'll never get another chance like this, I thought. But, in the long run, the Marshal's promise would matter little. It would be the shortest trial in history if I let him take me back, and I decided that I'd just as soon let it end here in the cave. And besides, as long as I was alive and free, there was always a chance that I might pay back a little on that debt that I owed to McCain and Slim Kasper. That alone was worth sticking it out. And Laura . . .

I didn't let myself think about Laura.

Mills shouted his promise again and I made no answer. Then, outside, we heard another sound, a new sound that hadn't been there before. A sound of hoofs in the distance. I went to the entrance of the cave and could see nothing, no sign of this new horseman, but I could hear Mills's men shuffling around, and a feeling of surprise and uneasiness hung on the morning air. Phil Carney came alert as he strained to hear.

"What do you make of it?"

"It sounds like somebody else has come to join the posse. Well, one more or less won't make much difference now."

There was loud arguing now, but the words were meaningless by the time they reached the cave. Among the voices there was one pitched higher than the others, and I thought for a moment that it was a woman's voice. But that was impossible, I told myself.

Once again I had forgotten that the impossible was a Carney stock in trade. "Carney!" It was the Marshal again. "Your sister's here. You don't want her to see you killed, do you?"

Laura here! It surprised Phil Carney as much as it did me. He grunted one savage curse and stepped close to the mouth of the cave, looking carefully around the clay edge. "Goddamnit, Marshal!" he shouted angrily. "Get my sister out of here!"

But I gathered that the Marshal had little to say about it. She was her brother's keeper, and nobody could change that, not even Silas Mills. I looked at Phil Carney and he was standing rigidly by the mouth of the cave. He needed no keeper now. He was a man, capable of paying his own debts in his own way—but I had no hope that Laura would ever understand that he had finally grown up.

And I guess Phil Carney was thinking the same thing. He said, with a curious absence of emotion in his voice, "I might have guessed that Laura would figure out a way to get me out of this. She's always got me out of things like this, ever since we were kids." He paused, looking thoughtfully at his rifle. "Well, by God, a time comes when a man has to take care of himself!"

Then he raised the rifle and fired one crashing shot through the opening of the cave.

For just a moment he stood there. "This is one time, Laura, that you won't be able to help me!"

Almost immediately the whole brushland to the right of us broke into a clatter of rifle fire. McCain had seen his chance and had taken it. Carney had fired the first shot; that was all the excuse he needed.

Laura's voice was lost in the noise now, and McCain and the Marshal were bringing their men around so they could shoot straight through that tunnel-like cave of ours. Phil Carney, ignoring the rock breastwork that he had built, stood in the opening firing as fast as he could jack cartridges into the chamber of his rifle. There was no time for anger now. There was only time for fighting, and there wouldn't be much for that.

Outside, I heard a man howl. Phil Carney laughed shortly. "That's one rider McCain can mark off his payroll!" Then a bullet burned into the cave and there was a sickening *spat* as I turned just in time to see the kid go down to one knee.

"That goddamn McCain!" he gritted, holding his leg where bright blood was spreading over the faded blue of his trousers.

I said, "Sit down. Let me have a look at it."

"There's no time for that!" He shoved me away and lurched to his feet. Then, before there was a chance of stopping him, he grabbed up his rifle and ran from the cave.

I heard the Marshal yell, "Hold your fire, it's the Carney kid!" But that didn't stop McCain and his boys. I guess the gambler figured that it was time to stop playing with Phil; the best way to take care of a hothead like that was to kill him. And that was what they were trying to do.

McCain had moved his men up close, trying to get them on the blind side of the cave, and seeing the kid running at them must have startled them. The Marshal was still yelling at them to hold their fire, and McCain and Kasper were yelling at them to shoot, and the men hesitated for a moment before deciding that they'd better listen to McCain and let the Marshal go. By this time Phil Carney had almost run down the barrels of their rifles— and suddenly he disappeared. I thought that one of McCain's men had brought him down for good until I saw him come into view again, and then I realized that he had fallen into a gully. He ran limping parallel to the gully for maybe three steps, and I thought: Doesn't the the crazy fool know he's been shot? Then he dived into the gully and there was a howl, and there was no way of knowing what had happened.

I must have acted on instinct alone. If I had stopped to reason, I would have stayed there in the cave and brought down as many as I could before they got me. But I didn't stop to reason. The next thing I knew, I was running after the kid.

I guess the Marshal thought we'd both gone crazy, or else he was too surprised to give his men the order to start shooting. Anyway, no fire came from Mills's direction. But McCain's men made up for it. I hit the ground on my belly and skidded under a blackjack, but the protection was too flimsy there and I began crawling. I kept crawling and finally one of those many gullies opened up in front of me and I fell into it.

Where Phil Carney was, I didn't know. I shouted, but there was no answer except for another volley from McCain's men, which went harmlessly over my head. Then I heard the sound of grunting and scuffling from somewhere up the draw, and I began crawling in that direction.

Just as I rounded a bend I saw what was happening. Phil Carney and Slim Kasper were grappling in the red clay dirt at the bottom of the wash. The kid was on his back, trying to hold Kasper's right hand in the two of his. But Phil Carney had lost a lot of blood by now and it was beginning to tell, and that hand was getting closer and closer to his throat. In Kasper's hand there was a knife.

I knelt frozen for one long second, held there by some terrible fascination as the knife moved down, down. And then at the last moment I felt the butt of my revolver in my hand.

When I pulled the trigger, Kasper slammed back as though he had been hit with a hammer. In my white-hot hate I had meant to kill him, but the bullet went astray and plowed into his shoulder. Still, I had only one idea in my head, and that was to kill him.

I guess the gambler knew what was in my mind. He had lost his own gun somewhere— maybe the kid had taken it away from him. Anyway, he was unarmed now, and those eyes of his were full of animal-like fear.

"For God's sake, Denfield! I'm not armed!"

"Neither was Kate Masters!" I said.

If it hadn't been for Phil Carney, I would have pulled the trigger again, because that was the only thing I could think of.

"Jeff, stop it!"

"This is my party, kid. This time you're not invited."

"Goddamn it, Jeff, Kasper's the only man that can save you!"

The words hung there, then they hit me. For once in his life, Phil Carney was right. Outside our gully hell was about to break loose. McCain was yelling that the kid and I had killed Kasper and for the Marshal to bring in his men and close in on us.

Then I shouted, "Kasper's not dead! But he will be, Marshal, if you move in here and start shooting!"

That gave them something to think about. None of them wanted to be personally responsible for a man's death. But I knew that wouldn't hold them for long.

"Denfield," the Marshal called angrily, "you and Carney come out of there! There'll be no lynching. You'll get a trial in Sabina."

"A trial wouldn't do me any good, with the evidence you think you've got against me," I called back. "I want to add to that evidence. Slim Kasper does, rather."

McCain didn't like this new turn that things had taken.

"Marshal," he yelled, "don't let that murderin' bastard make a fool out of you! Close in from your side and we'll smoke them out!"

"Marshal," I called, "do you want to hear Kasper's side of the story?"

There was a long moment of silence. McCain started yelling again, but Mills cut him off with an angry growl. Then he said tightly, "All right, Denfield. You get one minute, and then we're comin' after you."

I turned to Slim Kasper. "The rest is up to you. Do you want to tell the Marshal how Kate Masters died?"

"You're crazy!" he gasped, but he was scared.

"All right," I said, "it doesn't make much difference to me. If you'd rather die here . . ." I moved closer, on my knees, and put the revolver in his face, close enough so that he could smell the burned powder on the muzzle. Then I began pulling the trigger, very slowly.

"For God's sake, Denfield!"

"Do you want to talk?"

"What I'd say wouldn't help you! They wouldn't believe it in court!"

"Have it your own way," I said. My trigger finger was still applying pressure, and Kasper's face was covered with sweat.

"All right!" he gasped. "Take that pistol out of my face!"

I didn't ease up on the trigger, but I didn't apply any more pressure.

"Now tell the Marshal how Kate Masters died."

"I . . . killed her."

"Louder," I said. "I want the Marshal to hear this."

"I killed her," he said desperately, louder this time.

"What with?"

"With your gun. That old Griswold and Grier."

Phil Carney, very pale now, spoke for the first time. "Why?" he said. "Didn't McCain put you up to it? Wasn't it because Kate knew about the robbery, because she had helped McCain pull it off, and McCain sent you to keep an eye on her?"

In his desperation, Slim Kasper thought he saw

a way out. "Yeah!" he said quickly. "That's right! It was McCain's doin', all of it!"

"Marshal!" It was McCain this time, and his voice was near panic pitch. "Silas, you can't believe a word of what a man says when he's got a pistol against his head! You'd be a fool to listen to that kind of—"

Silas Mills cut him off coldly. "That'll do, McCain!"

From the gully we could hear nothing, but the shouting voices came clearly across the wasteland. Kasper was clutching his wounded shoulder, making small whimpering sounds as the sweat kept streaming down his face. He was in a bad spot—maybe even a worse spot than I was in—and he knew it. In the back of my mind I was aware of McCain and the Marshal arguing, but it was of little interest to me now because I was getting another idea.

I said, "Kasper, were you with McCain's boys when they broke into Stella's place?"

"No. So help me, Denfield, I had nothin' to do with it!"

I began applying slow pressure with my trigger finger. The hammer was ready to snap. I could feel it. But this was a gamble that there was no backing out of. Then Kasper's mouth began working frantically.

"All right, all right!" It was almost a sob. "I was with them!"

"Then you must know where McCain hid the gold. Where is it?"

His legs stiffened, as though he were trying to push himself through the dirt wall of the gully. "McCain would kill me!"

"Would you rather I did it?"

Slim Kasper had no choice, and he realized it. His chin dropped on his chest as the nerve went out of him. "It's back at headquarters." It was almost a whisper. "In the feed shed. I saw him put it in a sack of oats that he keeps for the horses."

"Did anybody else see it?"

He shook his head.

A feeling of new life took hold of me as I called over the lip of the gully. "Marshal . . ." But that was as far as I got. McCain was thinking ahead of me now. He knew that they could never tie him up with Kate Masters' death, no matter what Kasper said, but that robbery was something else again. If Kasper told what he knew about that and the gold was found in his feed shed, his days in Sabina would be over. And Kasper was scared. He would talk and keep talking. But McCain thought he knew how to take care of that.

"By God, Silas," the gambler yelled, "I'm not goin' to sit here and wait for one of my men to get killed!" His voice rose to an almost shrill pitch. "Charge that gully, boys! Smoke that murderin' bastard out of there!"

It worked. McCain had managed to shut me off

before I could tell the Marshal about the gold. The sharp, earsplitting crack of rifles shattered the uneasy dawn as the gambler bullied his men into attacking our place in the gully. Silas Mills's mad bellowing sounded above the firing, but too late to do any good. McCain's one chance of survival lay in killing every man in that gully, including Kasper.

There was no place to run. The Marshal's men stood dazed, reluctant to fire on McCain's cow hands as they charged us. I fired one, two shots from my revolver, but the gambler had whipped his men to a fury and there was no stopping them. The kid stood on his one good leg, braced against the lip of the gully, using his rifle as a club as the first man leaped down on top of us.

Then McCain appeared on the edge of the wash, looking as big as a mountain as he crouched there, poised, for one brief second, a big converted .44-caliber revolver aimed at my chest. I wheeled to face him, but much too late. I heard a shattering explosion, knowing that I had turned too late. But the life-taking jar of a bullet did not come.

McCain's mouth came open in surprise. He took one step back and dropped his revolver. Then he began falling awkwardly, as though the bones in his legs had suddenly turned to water, and he went crashing down, sprawling on the edge of the wash. And only then did I realize that the fight was over and the morning was silent once again. Typically,

Silas Mills had seized control of the situation by himself, through one savage burst of action.

For a long, silent moment he said not a word. He stood behind us, dark with anger and hate, a big hog-leg revolver still smoking in one hand. His eyes were savage with hate as he stood spread-legged, daring us, any one of us, to make a move. "Goddamn you!" he said harshly. Not to me, or the kid, or McCain, or anybody else in particular. He took several deep breaths and his hugeness seemed to grow slightly smaller. At last he lifted his left hand slightly and the awed men of his posse came forward.

"Burt," he said without looking around, "you and Henry go back to headquarters and get a spring wagon. I reckon three of these bastards won't be able to ride." They didn't say a word, but turned to do as they were told.

Only then did I realize that McCain was not dead. He slowly began to move, but the Marshal paid no attention to him. Mills stared at Slim Kasper with a look that was past anger, past hate. As from a long way off I heard the sound of sobbing, and I said:

"You might tell her that her brother is all right."

Mills didn't even hear me. He kept staring at Kasper. The sweat kept streaming down Kasper's twitching face and he couldn't return the stare. Guilt was in his eyes, in his whimpering voice. I saw the Marshal's hand tighten around the hooked butt of his revolver; killing was in his eyes. But then a hopelessness seemed to seize him and revulsion shook his huge frame, and at last he shoved the revolver back in its holster.

I knew how the Marshal felt. The anger had burned itself out and had left nothing but emptiness in its place, and that's the way it was with me. I could look at McCain and Kasper and feel nothing. The ache for vengence was missing. After a while I moved over to Phil Carney, ripped one of the sleeves off his shirt, and bound it around his leg. It wasn't much of a job, but it would have to do until they got him to town.

He said, "I guess it's a little late to say I'm sorry."

I could think of nothing to say, so I stood up and climbed out of the gully. The Marshal was still staring down at Slim Kasper. Kasper was having a bad time. He looked as though he wanted to say something, and his mouth kept working, but no sound came out. In a kind of desperation he clutched his shoulder, watching with sick fascination as the blood oozed through his fingers.

"God's sake!" The words blurted out suddenly. "Somebody do somethin'! I'm bleedin' to death!"

Across the gully one of McCain's riders was binding up the gambler's leg, but no one made a move to help Kasper. "Honest to God!" he whined. "I didn't mean to kill her! She ran at me and the gun went off! Denfield saw it, he can tell you!"

Silas Mills straightened and quickly looked away. If there had been any doubt in his mind, it was gone now. He said harshly, "One of you men see if you can stop the bleedin'." And he turned and walked a few steps away so that he wouldn't have to look at Kasper's face. I wanted to say something to the Marshal, but I knew that words would be no good. He had been in love with a fancy girl and now she was dead. The bitterness was locked up inside him and there could be no relief. Only duty, as he saw it.

I walked away from the gully and no one tried to stop me. Then I walked over to where two men were holding Laura's arms and I said, "Let her go." And strangely enough, they did it.

She stood there for a moment, her eyes wide, and then, suddenly, somehow, she was in my arms. I said, "It's all right. Your brother's got a flesh wound in the leg, but he'll be riding again within a week or two."

"It was my fault, Jeff! It was all my fault!"

I didn't know what she meant. I only knew that the old excitement was still there when I had my arms around her, and I knew that my sickness was something that nothing could cure, because she had ruined me for all other women in the world.

She said, "I should have let him alone! I shouldn't have tried to boss him!"

And then I understood the way she was thinking. "Maybe," I said. "Anyway, I think your job is over now. If Phil still wants this ranch, I think McCain is in the mood to sell. Mills will never allow him to stay in Sabina after what's happened today. The stolen money is back at headquarters, in one of the feed sheds, according to Kasper; that will make a down payment. And I guess McCain will take it. He'll need the money for a lawyer, if he doesn't want to spend the rest of his life in prison." I breathed deeply, feeling a strange peace as I held her. I said, "I think your brother has grown up. Maybe someday he'll be the man your father was, but he'll have to manage it himself. Another person's sacrificing won't help him or make him better."

She dropped her head and was very quiet for a long moment. "And me?" she asked finally.

"You, Laura? Maybe you've grown up too."

Then the spring wagon came from headquarters and Phil Carney refused to ride with Kasper and McCain. He would be damned, he said, if he would ride with a thief and a murderer, but he was too weak to fight and they put him in anyway. Laura and I rode ahead of the wagon. She didn't want to look at McCain, and neither did I.

The Marshal kept me in Sabina for almost a week, asking angry questions and getting everything down in black and white, and finally he said that was all. I could go.

The day I had looked forward to had come at

last. I could go. I walked past the stage office, then I walked back and went in and told the old agent that I wanted two tickets to St. Louis. Maybe this would be the biggest fool thing I ever did, I told myself, but I might as well make the last one a big one.

That night, after supper was over at the Charleston House, I waited on the front porch until Laura came out, as she often did. She breathed deeply, enjoying the wild smell of sage in the evening air. I could think of no subtle way of saying the thing I had to say, so I showed her the two stage tickets and said:

"Will you come with me, Laura?"

For a moment I was afraid she wasn't going to answer. She came erect and kept staring out at the bleak brushland that she loved so much. Then, at last, she seemed to relax. "I was afraid you weren't going to ask me," she said quietly.

I hadn't expected it to be like that. No coaxing, no arguing. She added, "Of course I'll go with you, Jeff. Did you think I wouldn't?"

I was too stunned to feel anything just then. I couldn't believe that she completely understood what I was asking her to do.

"Jeff . . ." She was facing me, smiling. "For a long time I've had just one purpose in life, and that was to make my brother over in the image of my father. I wanted the Carney name to be big, to mean something, as it used to. Phil and I are more alike than I thought, I suppose. But I always thought of my brother as a headstrong boy, and it never occurred to me that he would be a man someday and wouldn't need me to look after him. That day has come, hasn't it, Jeff?"

"If it's ever to come."

She touched my face and I pulled her against me.

I said, "The river country isn't much like Sabina. Do you think you can be happy away from Texas?"

I knew that she had thought of that. For a long while, probably. And then she said, "But you won't change, will you, Jeff? That's the important thing."

"No," I said, "I guess I won't change much." But the time for talking was over. I held her hard against me, and a soft breeze came out of the south, bringing that wild Texas smell with it, and I knew that it would be a long time before I forgot what that country smelled like.

Center Point Large Print
600 Brooks Road / PO Box 1
Thorndike, ME 04986-0001 USA

(207) 568-3717

US & Canada:
1 800 929-9108
www.centerpointlargeprint.com